Ezra and Other Stories

Barbara A. Whittington

AUTHOR'S NOTE:

These stories are as varied as their name titles. Some came fully realized from the moment I first wrote their names on paper, such as "Wally and Bun," and "Vinnie." Others came from thinking of specific events such as the Kent State shootings in "Micro Wave." Some remain a mystery even to me. "Mabel and the Garage Sale" came from my pondering where people moved to when I-64 came through West Virginia taking their homes. "Mabel" was dramatized by British Broadcasting Corporation and aired world wide on National Public Radio. "Joy Ruth and Minnie Hendrix" appeared in The Writer's Magazine Issue #4 in the United Kingdom and is loosely based on the visit my mother and I made to the funeral home to make her arrangements. "Eve and Marcus Welby" was written as part of a Humanities class assignment; It found a home at Cat Fancy Magazine some years back. My hope is that you will enjoy reading these stories as much as I did writing them. Thank you to two great gals, Charlene and Darlene, for letting me use their names.

Dedicated to all the people from whom I've taken bits and pieces to create my characters and stories. Thanks to all my friends and family who continue to encourage my writing efforts. Much appreciation goes to my family in West Virginia who still love and support me, and to grandson Daniel Eltzroth for helping create my Ezra cover. Blessings!

"People are hungry for stories. It's part of our very being. Storytelling is a form of history, of immortality too. It goes from one generation to another." **Studs Terkel**

CONTENTS

Mabel and the Garage Sale

Interstate 64 is taking Mabel's house. The highway is slated to run south, through the middle of her living room, all the way to the ocean. Mabel figures the road will roll down right where the gold velvet love seat rests now. She gets uneasy thinking about it but it's too late. They have the house and Mabel has the money. All that's left is deciding where to go with it.

Her daughter, Donna Faye, has said she can move in with her. Mabel knows the girl isn't sincere so she is drawing out her last few days in the house, trying to decide what to do.

She has thought about renting one of the new brick garden apartments near the center of town except she isn't good with figures and has no idea how long $30,000 would run her.

To make matters worse, Mabel has something wrong with her back. She has been unable to work at the Holiday Inn, where some days she can clear $25 cleaning rooms. Since she stopped going to work her back hasn't bothered her much. If anything, it seems to be on the mend. It could be she's too preoccupied breaking up housekeeping to notice the pain.

Mabel considered living with her son, Jackie Lee, but his wife, Cindy Sue, would not agree to it. Besides, they live across the tracks in a house smaller than Mabel's and have three rowdy boys. It seems to Mabel she is between a rock and a hard place.

At the garage sale Mabel is having, her friend Maryann wants to buy her corn popper. In fact, Maryann starts loading up a box with things she wants to buy. In the box, she puts Mabel's corn popper, a heating pad with a blue flannel cover still in the original plastic, an orange heavy duty extension cord which Mabel bought at a garage sale and never used, several Tupperware bowls which are peeling and will no longer burp, and a new microwave cake pan which was Donna Faye's Christmas gift to Mabel. Mabel doesn't own a microwave.

"I'll give you two-dollars for this whole box," Maryann says, adding several Maxwell House coffee cans to the box as she talks. The cans have snow scenes and are priced at a quarter each. Mabel thought they would make someone nice cookie tins at Christmas.

"Sure," she says to Maryann, who has helped price everything for the sale.

Secretly, Mabel thinks Maryann is doing her dirty, especially in view of the fact she took the corn popper out of the hands of a heavy woman who was about ready to buy it. From the looks of the woman, she could afford to pay full-price, too, what with her spectator pumps, matching handbag, and all.

When there is a lull between customers, the two women carry a big box of dishes out of the house and into the yard. Mabel doesn't have a garage but to her a garage sale sounds better than a yard sale.

"I've never seen so much stuff," Maryann says, looking at the cluttered yard.

"Keep it you might need it," Mabel says, opening the box of dishes. "Something I learned at my daddy's knee."

In reality, Mabel never learned anything at her daddy's knee. He stayed drunk and didn't want any of his nine kids near him. It makes her feel good to say it to Maryann who has acted smart all day.

Maryann thinks she's something special. Mabel knows different. She knows Maryann had to marry Arnie Breedlove. The fact she lives in a pink ranch across town and Arnie's still around is incidental as far as Mabel is concerned.

Mabel puts out several of the china plates trimmed in pink roses. The set isn't complete but would do someone just starting out. Maryann wheels Donna Faye's old red bike out of the shed.

They had to move Jackie Lee's little blue scooter to get the bike through the door. Mabel has been ignoring the scooter but realizes she has got to stop holding stuff back. She carries the scooter out into the yard and puts it alongside the bike.

Maryann has a table set up for her knickknacks. She is rearranging them, putting the coconut with the monkey's face out front. She is tired of using it as a door stop. She hopes it will bring fifty cents.

Mabel has a clothesline strung from the shed to the house. On it she hangs some polyester pantsuits to replace the ones she sold the day before. She doesn't mind selling the suits cheap. She picks them up for nearly nothing down at Goodwill. She hangs other odds and ends on the line.

When Mabel walks over to help a fat woman in an orange muu muu try the hot curlers in her hair, she sees Maryann going through the clothes on the line. Maryann pulls at some clothes wedged between a pair of old coveralls and a worn-out shirt Mabel felt would make someone a good cleaning rag.

Until the garage sale, Mabel hadn't done much house cleaning. The whole business has inspired her and she has scrubbed every room in the house with Murphy's Oil Soap. She wants it clean when she leaves.

Just the other night she dreamed that the supervisor of the I-64 crew walked through the house one last time and came out saying it was all a big mistake and that I-64 wasn't coming anywhere near her house. She woke in a cold sweat, the smell of Murphy's Oil Soap heavy in the air.

"Mabel Jenkins," Maryann is squealing, "where did you get hold of a coat like this?" Maryann is holding a black velvet jacket up to her and is twirling around the yard. Her yellow skirt is ballooning around her long skinny legs, revealing a run in her panty hose. The jacket is the same ink-black as Maryann's long dyed hair.

"Give me that," Mabel says and jerks the coat from MaryAnn.

Mabel got the coat at the city dump the same day she found the 9 x 12 rug which is avocado green and in her living room now. She isn't telling Maryann. She wants Maryann to think she bought the coat for some fancy doings. Maryann is forever bragging about the time she wore her sister's fox trimmed jacket to a gospel singing at the Civic Center.

Mabel tries to ease the tension. "I got a lot riding on this coat, honey," she says. She brushes the coat and returns it to the clothesline. "It's the nicest thing I got to sell. I got it marked $20. I need $10 out of it. Think I can get it?"

Maryann is clearly miffed. She ignores Mabel's outstretched hand and goes about setting up a table for her glassware. Glassware usually sells well. Maryann has a set of plastic Smurf cups her cousin brought her from Canada. She suspects her cousin got them free with Cokes. She puts the plastic cups behind the set of glasses she bought when IGA was running a special. They are good quality. Maryann picks up one and inspects it. The glass is clear, with orange flowers trailing around the rim. Maryann hums as she works, arranging the various pieces of glassware.

Mabel goes inside to bring the last box from the attic. She thinks the house appears lighter and more airy now that she has gotten rid of so much stuff. Soon all her things will be gone and then she too will have to go. Every time she thinks of moving she gets a sick feeling in the pit of her stomach. If only Donna Faye hadn't grown up to be so different. They might have been friends. Instead, her daughter has married a doctor and lives with him in a big house out in the country. They have no children and Donna Faye takes music and voice lessons.

Outside, Mabel goes through the cardboard box. On top of some old photo albums, she runs across a baseball cap that belonged to Spook Lanham. Spook Lanham was not Donna Faye's daddy, though he thought he was when he married Mabel over in Maryland. Mabel thought so too.

Donna Faye has a high IQ and she didn't get it from Spook. Mabel figures she got it from the Bible salesman who stayed with them while he worked the town. He had to sleep on the couch in the living room. This was during the time Mabel's mother joined the Fifth Avenue Baptist Church and went to services three nights a week and twice on Sunday.

Mabel was sixteen and didn't know what hit her. She blamed it on his looks. Tall, dark, and handsome, and the animated way he had of talking about them living by the ocean someday. He was the smartest person Mabel had ever met. It wasn't long before she was taking him for rides in her mother's old Chevy, riding clear out to Tucker's Creek and not getting home until daylight.

One day Mabel came home from the drugstore where she worked that summer and the Bible salesman was gone. Mabel had assumed when he moved on he'd take her with him.

It didn't work out that way. All he took with him was her dream of seeing the ocean.

She finds several more ball caps belonging to Spook Lanham. Way down in one corner of the box of junk, she uncovers the ring that Hank, the Bible salesman, gave her on one of those moonlit nights out at Tucker's Creek.

Later in the day, Mabel sells the ring for a quarter to a pimply faced kid. The ring was on the table alongside Spook's ball caps. The kid bought the caps too, stacking them all on his head at one time. He reminded Mabel of a monkey she once saw on Captain Kangaroo.

Spook Dwight Lanham had come into Mabel's life just as the Bible salesman was leaving. Spook's real name was Dwight but everyone called him Spook because he lived out by the cemetery. Mabel took him out to Tucker's Creek a few times in her mother's Chevy and then she married him. Donna Faye was not yet two when Spook went out walking on the railroad track one dark night and got run over by a train.

Jackie Lee Jenkins, the third man in Mabel's life and the second one she married, was as good-looking as sin itself. He hung around only long enough to seduce the wife of the choir director at the Fifth Avenue Baptist Church. All this under the pretense of being born again.

At least from that marriage Mabel got her son, Jackie Lee Junior and the five-room house which I-64 will soon take. The house was a present from Granny Jenkins for all Mabel had been through.

"It's the devil in him," Granny said, every time Mabel went to visit her at the nursing home. She was proud as a peacock of Jackie Lee Junior. Back before Granny ever got sick, he painted her VW candy apple red and wouldn't let her give him a dime.

"Nothing like his daddy," Granny said to Mabel a thousand times. When she died she left the VW to Mabel. However Mabel cannot drive a stick shift. The car is parked on the street where it's been since the funeral.

The garage sale is dead now except for some neighborhood kids hanging around Maryann's knickknack table. Mabel goes into the basement and brings up another box. She isn't sure what is in it but she sets it on the grass next to an empty table and lifts the dusty lid.

After a leggy spider crawls from the box, Mabel lifts out an apple peeler and a paddle for a butter churn. She smiles. These are items she brought from her grandmother's farm when it was sold. Something tells Mabel the items are money makers. She will put them on a separate table to attract serious buyers. She couldn't imagine putting a paddle for a butter churn next to a metal ice tray which is selling for 10 cents. Mabel busies herself printing new signs.

Maryann's boy, Jeff, stopped by earlier to check on the progress of the garage sale and to leave a box of Little Debbie oatmeal cakes to tide the women over until supper. Mabel thinks Jeff is a good boy though she would never tell Maryann. She hasn't seen hide nor hair of her own children. Donna Faye has her lessons and Jackie Lee paints cars from dawn to dusk. Mabel sees her daughter-in-law, Cindy Sue, drive by with the boys mid afternoon. She's glad Cindy Sue doesn't stop. Those demon-boys would destroy her whole garage sale in one swipe.

When the pickup with the camper pulls into the yard, Mabel is giving change to a young woman in jogging clothes who bought Donna Faye's bike. Mabel is surprised someone wanted it. The chain is broken and the fenders are rusted. As the young woman wheels the bike away, Mabel gets lightheaded thinking how quickly things are moving.

Maryann has struck up a conversation with the man in the pickup truck. Both women have learned that in order to sell stuff, you have to mix with the people.

The man, who looks vaguely familiar to Mabel, doesn't ask for tools or lawn mowers. He goes straight to the clothesline and starts going through the clothes.

"Do you have any clothes for a little girl," he asks.

"No," Mabel says, figuring he will leave. Instead he wants the history of each item of clothing.

"Who does this belong to?"

"Where'd you wear this?"

"Does this have a jacket to match?"

Mabel, who is nearby dusting a floor lamp, answers his questions and the man moves deeper into the clothes on the line.

He pulls out a three-piece wool pantsuit and holds it up for closer inspection. "This new?"

Mabel laughs. "It made me itch. I never wore it."

Mabel has never met a man quite like this one. She can't put her finger on what it is about him that sets him apart.

He picks out a dress for his sister, a navy blue polyester knit with splashy white flowers, and the pair of coveralls for his brother-in-law to wear when he "jimmies around the garage." He has kept a running conversation with Mabel, telling her finally he was a year ahead of her in school, and his eyes shine. He gathers up the Smurf glasses for his niece.

Maybe it is because he's so open that Mabel is drawn to him. Or maybe it is because he turns to her every little bit asking her advice and then listens while she gives it. At some point he touches her shoulder and Mabel likes this. She is sorry she cannot remember him from school.

He spends $20 buying all kinds of gadgets. He doesn't dicker as some people do. This pleases Mabel. He buys the apple peeler and the butter paddle. After saying several times he'd better be going, he heads over to the blue pickup and puts his bags on the front seat. Then, he waves Mabel over to the new camper and asks if she would like to see inside.

Mabel looks around the yard. There isn't a soul at the garage sale. Maryann might object but she's gone home. Mabel goes over and steps up into the camper. Her feet sink into plush blue carpet that matches the velvet curtains. Even the seats of the dinette set are blue velvet. The little walnut table will seat only two. Mabel especially loves the bunk beds built into the wall. She thinks the camper must have cost a lot of money but Ralph seems like a regular guy.

"You won't believe this," Ralph finally says. He has asked her to call him Ralph. She sits down across from him at the table. He has opened a Coke for her and a Little King for himself.

"You won't believe this," he says again, and then he clears his throat. "I won the lottery - a million bucks." He laughs. "Now what does a guy who's never had a dime, do with a million bucks?"

He keeps on laughing and Mabel isn't sure what to make of the story he's telling.

She smiles, though, because she likes Ralph.

"I don't even like money," Ralph says, between laughs.

Mabel notices a sack of old clothes in the corner of the camper and wonders if she has gotten mixed in with some kind of garage sale nut.

Ralph looks as if he might burst into tears. He goes quiet, then he says slowly, "I'm thinking of going out west." He clears his throat and looks at her. "Yes, I'm going out west." He stares at Mabel intently.

She sips her Coke and nods at the man across from her.

"I'd like to take you with me."

Mabel sees herself in the mirror above the table. She is pleased with her reflection. Her brown hair is only slightly streaked with gray. Her cheeks are pink.

"I'm serious, Mabel," Ralph says, "I've got to pack me up a few things. Say the word and I'll come back by and get you. What do you say?"

Mabel smiles at him. After she promises to think about his offer, he downs the rest of his Little King and helps her out of the camper.

When he is gone, she sits in her webbed lawn chair for a long time watching the dusk gather around her. She decides the garage sale has run its course. She is tired. It is time, she feels, to move on to something else.

She will learn to drive Granny's VW and take all the leftover junk to the dump. That will leave the house empty. Ready for the bulldozers. Ready for I-64.

Maryann has offered Mabel a place to stay until she gets her footing but Mabel can't help but think it's because she is giving Maryann the gold velvet love seat and the piece of green carpet.

She decides she will not tell Maryann her plans. This gives her a good feeling and she hums to herself as she folds up her chair. She isn't scared anymore.

If Ralph comes back, she just might go with him. She can send everyone a postcard from somewhere far off. Maybe from one of the national parks. Yellowstone, maybe. She can send them all a picture of a bear or of Old Faithful.

If Ralph doesn't come back, she'll gather up her life and get on with things. She can always go back to the Holiday Inn. Just the other day the head of housekeeping called and wanted her back. She might even move over there.

Or she might use the money to buy herself a pickup. Or maybe a van. She can travel and see things she's only dreamed about. Yes. That's what she will do. Buy herself a van. And head it south, down I-64, toward the ocean.

Delphine and Rainelle

Every weekday morning Delphine and Rainelle meet in Rainelle's kitchen at 9 a.m. After 20 years it is a ritual. At exactly five of nine, after reading the Gazette, more specifically working the crossword puzzle - she is good with words - Delphine walks three houses down the street to Rainelle's door where her friend is brewing a fresh pot of coffee from the Columbian beans she buys at Kroger's every Friday and grinds herself.

They don't discuss it but Rainelle's place is the nicest by far. Bud has just remodeled the kitchen. He's put up new wallpaper and installed walnut-finish cabinets, stainless steel sink with disposal, and a no-wax Solarian floor in Morning Meadow pattern. It's blue and beige with the tiniest flowers.

The minute Rainelle mentioned having the kitchen done over Bud said to call J.C. Penney's and order everything. Delphine and Rainelle spent weeks poring over the catalogues, picking out the stuff. Delphine feels the kitchen is almost hers.

It was an accident, the last time Delphine's own kitchen got something new. Charlie was driving through Hunting Hills on his way home from the plant. He says seeing all those manicured lawns, one right after the other, clears his head. It was there that he found the carpet, blue with a bright rainbow running across the center, there at the end of one of those long winding driveways. It only took him a jiffy to load it into his Luv truck. Charlie has muscles galore.

Charlie has picked up discards out there before. But nothing near as nice as the rug. Charlie is a recycler from the word go. He brought that rug home, rolled it out right in the kitchen, it was a perfect fit, and it's been there ever since. Charlie is funny. He likes nice things but he's just as happy when they belong to someone else. Charlie is the exact opposite of Bud.

After coffee, the two women sometimes go to the Community Center where they do ceramics. They are working on an elaborate nativity scene which they intend to share but haven't worked out the details. Rainelle says Delphine is turning Mary's lips into a pout by not painting in the lines. Delphine has offered the brush to Rainelle who refuses to do any of the close work. So, until they can get Mary right they are at a standstill on the project. Not that there's any hurry. It is only March.

It's a Monday. Rainelle is pouring them a second cup of coffee from the new Mr. Coffee she bought on sale last week in White's. That's one thing about Rainelle. She buys on sale.

"I love that wallpaper," Delphine says, running her fingers along the row of stenciled houses that border the wallpaper in the alcove where Rainelle has her new solid oak table and 6 chairs.

It seems to Rainelle that Delphine has made that remark about the wallpaper at least ten times this morning. Maybe it's just her nerves. They are ready to give.

As she refills the cream pitcher, Rainelle stares out the bay window at the plastic Easter eggs littering the back yard. In all the years she has decorated the little tree, the eggs have never blown off. Not once. She shudders as she stirs Coffee Rich into her coffee. She read somewhere that Coffee Rich was better for you than the powdered stuff. Less cholesterol. At the moment she doesn't give a damn about cholesterol. Something awful is going to happen. No. Something awful has already happened.

This morning Melanie Hook called at 8:07 a.m. Just before Rainelle had finished reading Dear Abby. A man was asking Abby's advice on bringing his second wife to his daughter's wedding. He said his daughter had dared him to bring "that crumb" and his first wife was threatening to blow up the church. Well, blowing up the church was too good for that woman. Rainelle could think of better words than crumb, too.

She let the phone ring and ring hoping whoever was calling would get tired and hang up. She figured it was Delphine who sometimes called to see what Rainelle was wearing that day. In spite of the fact she was a heavy woman, Rainelle knew how to dress. She could blend colors and she wore scarves and belts to accent her outfits. She wasn't afraid to be bold. She learned most of it from Beeline clothes. She had held home parties for a year or two and then gave it up for Avon. Delphine tries to imitate Rainelle's style by wearing large belts and bright colored scarves with everything.

"Hello," she finally said into the phone, agitated at the disruption. She had planned to surprise Delphine with a Bisquick coffee cake but wouldn't have time now.

It was Melanie Hook from Circle. Melanie whose husband, Everett, works in the shoe department at Sears and wears burgundy polyester suits and shiny white loafers year round. Melanie who thinks she owns Circle because she opens her home, the only split level in town, for every holiday and goes all out at Christmas with a buffet. Rainelle could take Melanie Hook or leave her. This particular morning she would rather leave her.

Melanie had spoken only a few words when Rainelle felt herself getting sick. It was a sick that turned her insides out. She's only felt this way one other time. It was on her sixteenth birthday, the day she found out she was pregnant. And now this morning at 8:07.

"I might be wrong," Melanie said, "but I don't think so. Unless Bud has a double. What was odd," she said, pausing to take a deep breath, "was he was sitting there in the Red Lobster in that new gray suit of his with a girl no older than your Linda. Holding hands in, well, in an intimate way."

Rainelle remembered last summer. Linda was a sight to see in her white wedding gown holding onto Bud's arm as they both smiled into the camera. The guests bragged as much on Bud that afternoon as they did on Linda. Rainelle gave him credit. They had been going to Weight Watcher's and he had lost 50 pounds. Rainelle had not lost an ounce. Now that he was using that comb-in hair color he looked ten years younger. The other thing people bragged on that day was Bud's new gray suit. Maybe she was just jealous. Not one person commented on her floor-length turquoise dress or about her hair which she'd had highlighted at J.C. Penney's just for the wedding.

Melanie Hook kept talking but Rainelle wasn't sure what she was saying. She was about to throw up. She saw her form waver as she looked down at the shiny kitchen floor. "No more waxing!" "No more waxing!" kept playing in her head like a commercial gone awry. She felt the way she'd always thought she'd feel if she ever fell out of an airplane.

"I guess Bud wouldn't be up in Charleston on a week night," Melanie said after what seemed like forever, "not in the rain, anyway. It was raining like the devil that night. Did I ever tell you how much I loved Linda's wedding?" Melanie's voice droned on. "That watermelon basket you made was something. And those pink crocheted nut cups. Cute! Rainelle, are you still there? Look, let's forget I called. I'm too impulsive. Everett says I am. Too impulsive for my own good."

"All I know is," Rainelle said, before hanging the white receiver onto the wall phone by the new range, "it wasn't Bud." In Charleston. And in the rain. Bud went to Union meetings. In Charleston. Sometimes it rained.

Just last week Bud had asked where she wanted to go on vacation this year. He had two weeks coming up. He'd walked in from work, set his lunch pail on the sink and come up behind her, hugging her as he asked.

"Myrtle Beach," she had said automatically, not because she wanted to go there but because that's where they always went.

At the dinner table that evening as they ate beef stew and her specialty, Angel Biscuits, Bud had asked Missy and Jeffy the same question and they had both squealed, "Myrtle Beach!" They loved that place. Bud always splurged and got a place on the ocean. Rainelle wasn't much for the water. She liked to walk along the beach when it was deserted looking for shells. As far as Bud was concerned the beach was for getting a tan. He spent hours covered with tropical oil stretched out on a towel in the sand, sunglasses perched on his nose, a can of beer in one hand and *Sports Illustrated* in the other.

He also liked to hit the souvenir shops. He came home every year with a Myrtle Beach t-shirt. Bud wore nothing but tight fitting jeans and t-shirts. He went in for seashell lamps, too, and ash trays with flamingos in the center. The shop off the garage was filled with his mementos and his girlie calendars.

Rainelle would stay in their room at the beach and read. She had read every book Danielle Steel had ever written. She watched re-runs of Wheel of Fortune. She loved Vanna White's clothes. Rainelle was good at outguessing the contestants on the show, too.

Or she would just walk up and down the strip and listen. She had always been interested in what other people had to say. She especially liked to eavesdrop on couples. That's how she measured her life with Bud. She always seemed to come out ahead. Funny, though. It didn't make her feel any better.

Some days Rainelle talked to the maid who cleaned their rooms. Once she even got supplies off the cart and cleaned their room herself, changing the sheets and putting out clean towels. It gave her a sense of purpose. Too, it kept her mind from thinking things she didn't want to think. That was the bad thing about vacations. There was too much time to think.

On this day she can't seem to let go of Melanie Hook's words. All through coffee and even the Baklava that Delphine brought, she hears, "The girl was no older than Linda." Those are the words that cause Rainelle the most pain.

At the Community Center, Delphine labors over Mary while Rainelle tells her everything Melanie Hook said. Delphine goes right on working on Mary, moving the tiny paint brush first this way and then that. She is like that. When it is anything important she takes her time answering. If she ever does.

The room is silent except for an occasional round of applause from the cake decorating class down the hall. There, the instructor is putting the finishing touches on a wedding cake with a fountain.

With Melanie's words racing around in her head Rainelle goes down the hall to get a Coke. She puts 5 dimes and a nickel in the machine and as the can falls she presses her cheek to the cold machine and wonders how she will ever get through the day.

Rumors had flown around town once before. Bud was involved with an office girl at the plant. Nothing ever came of it. She ran into the girl once. It was Jeffy's eighth birthday and the party was at McDonald's. She bumped into her, Mary something, and the girl had turned and fled. She watched Bud during that time. There was never a sign. If anything he was more attentive. And he took up calling her Baby again. That had been his name for her, Baby, when they first got married. It was because Linda was on the way before the wedding. He was proud of the fact. Rainelle could never understand why. At least he only called her Baby when they were alone. Even then it made her feel kind of silly.

She sips on the Coke and watches Delphine dab at Mary's delicate face with the tiny paint brush. Unable to stand the quiet any longer, she blurts out, "It isn't true, Delphine, what Melanie Hook is saying about Bud. She's a liar. She's a liar, and you know she is!"

Delphine raises an eyebrow and gives Rainelle a look that says she believes every word Melanie Hook is saying. The looks says, "You know it too, Rainelle. Wake up!"

The silence screams at Rainelle. She closes her eyes and puts her head down on the table between them. She feels anger seeping from Delphine's very pores. Surely Delphine should know by now. Waking up is not an option for Rainelle.

On the trip home, both women are silent.

Later, Rainelle cuts a coupon for Blue Bonnet Margarine from the newspaper. Her mother uses Blue Bonnet and Rainelle has never bought anything else. Now she is stretched out in her Laz-E-Boy recliner surrounded by her collection of Avon decanters. She had to quit selling Avon because of the decanters. They ate up her profit.

This is the one place in the whole house that brings her comfort. She takes her time organizing her coupon box, separating the ones she doesn't use. She is taking them to the meeting Tuesday night. She belongs to the Krazy Klippers Koupon Club which meets in the basement of the Lutheran Church. She is president.

She turns the newspaper to her horoscope. She is a Sagittarius. Her birthday is December 1st. "You have a chance to come from behind and win the whole ball game. Weigh all sides before making an important decision. Plan a journey." She cuts out her horoscope and then reads Delphine's. Delphine is a Gemini, born on June 12th. "Do all those little things that need doing," she reads, "get organized. Be honest when it comes to a good friend. Let the chips fall where they may." She cuts out the horoscope for Delphine, highlighting in yellow "get organized," and sticks it next to hers on the refrigerator with a teddy bear magnet.

Delphine is the most disorganized person Rainelle knows. There isn't a place to sit down in her whole house. She loves home parties and has stacks and stacks of Tupperware and Rubbermaid on every chair. The stuff has even spilled out into her living room.

Delphine and Charlie eat out every night. Why she buys so many bowls and food containers nobody knows. She is good to loan out things, like her cake taker and lettuce keeper, and she gives the stuff as gifts.

Rainelle has several pieces she's borrowed and never returned. Delphine gave Linda enough stuff to fill her car trunk the day of Linda's wedding shower. She even threw in some gadgets she'd ordered from Walter Drake. Two were things Linda loved. Plastic hooks to dry pantyhose over the shower and burner covers with snow scenes. That same day Delphine gave Rainelle a silver tea egg and a silver spoon rest. She is a good-hearted person. Linda is fixed for life on some of her kitchen things.

Rainelle didn't set up her own kitchen until long after Linda was born. They stayed with Bud's mom that first year. It was when she was setting up her kitchen that she'd overheard the remarks. It was in the pots and pans section in Woolworth's. She wasn't sure it was her Bud they were discussing, the two women from church, but she'd heard "Bud," and "fooling with," and they had clammed up when they caught sight of her. She'd walked away, her head held high. That was the first and only time she ever confronted Bud with anything she had heard. That was when she got pregnant with Jeffy. He was their accident.

"Baby, you don't believe those small-minded biddies. Baby, come here," he'd said after she told him what they said. "Poor baby to have to hear that kind of stuff. No wonder you're upset," he said and held her tighter and tighter and pulled her over to the bed.

She'd gotten pregnant with Jeffy right then and there and she'd had to put all her suspicions behind her. Right after that they changed churches, from Methodist to Presbyterian, and she felt better all the way around. The day she had Jeffy christened she knew as she watched Bud holding the baby she'd done the right thing.

After putting away the newspaper and coupons, Rainelle can't seem to settle down to anything else. She straightens pictures, waxes furniture that already shines and rearranges the magnets on the refrigerator door. She adds several more teddy bear magnets to the horoscopes on the door to keep them from sliding down. She puts Delphine's horoscope in easy view. She wants her to see it first thing.

But Delphine doesn't come to Rainelle's for coffee the next day. Or the next. Or the day after that. She doesn't call either. She finally sends word through Charlie at the plant that she wants Rainelle to keep her cake taker and the lettuce keeper. One evening, out of the blue, Charlie shows up at their door with a Tupperware ball for the baby Linda is expecting in the fall. He stays for coffee but doesn't mention Delphine's name.

Rainelle knows she will be back. She always comes back. Sooner or later. The last time Rainelle looked the other way, Delphine said, "You can only be run over so many times by a train, Rainelle. Sooner or later there will be nothing left of you. Get off that track, girl!"

A month passes. Rainelle finally leaves word at the Community Center that the nativity scene should be given to Delphine. It has been her project all along.

In May, Rainelle begins to pack for Myrtle Beach. She starts way ahead giving herself plenty of time. Bud goes out to the car dealer and buys a new car. It is blue. He says blue is Rainelle's color. She does love the car, especially the plush seats. It is their first convertible. Until their vacation, Bud is driving the new car and Rainelle is driving Bud's Chevette. Bud says he wants to break in the new car before their trip.

One morning Rainelle drives by Delphine's house. She sees the Volunteers of America loading a truck with boxes of Tupperware and Rubbermaid. She sees Delphine standing on a ladder cleaning the front window. Charlie is pruning bushes. He is bare to the waist and sweat glistens on his back. They don't see Rainelle as she drives past.

Later that week Delphine and Charlie both see Bud. They are walking into McDonald's over in Putnam County near the 84 Lumber where they've gone to buy some paneling. Delphine is fussing with the fuchsia neck scarf Rainelle gave her for her last birthday.

It is lunch time and the place is crowded. Delphine is telling Charlie she might join the Krazy Klippers Klub. Rainelle is on her mind, has been since she picked up the nativity scene at the Community Center. "Yes," she repeats opening the door of McDonald's, "I'm gonna give those Krazy Klippers a whirl."

"Good idea," Charlie says patting her on the shoulder and then stops in his tracks, his large frame half in and half out of the door.

They both see Bud at the same time. He is at the drive-thru window. The top is down on the new car.

"Got a bad desire," Bruce Springsteen wails from Bud's car radio, "I'm on Fire." The girl sitting next to Bud is laughing up into his face.

Charlie orders, collects the food, and leads Delphine to a booth by the window. The Big Macs go untouched as they watch a smiling Bud drive away, one arm wrapped around the steering wheel of Rainelle's new convertible and one arm wrapped around the young girl. A girl no older than Linda.

Delphine calls Rainelle, the minute she gets home. But Rainelle will not let her get a word in edgewise. Rainelle has been to Charleston to J. C. Penney's. Bud is letting her re-do their bedroom. In shades of blue.

Hoot and Marla

Hoot and Marla are on their way to Niagara Falls. Hoot's sister, Betty Sue, has talked Hoot into letting her come. She has brought along her boyfriend, Nick.

Hoot is driving the black Monte Carlo he bought last week for $800. Everyone is to chip in on the gas.

"All-my-x's-live-in-Tex-as," Hoot sings along with the radio, "that's why I hang my hat in Tennessee!" He taps his hand on the steering wheel in time to the music.

Hoot loves George Strait. Not as much as he loves Elvis though. Hoot is an Elvis Presley look alike. He's never traded on it or anything. But he can sing and play the guitar, too. Marla nearly dies when he sings, "Love me Tender." He's that good.

Now, as he sings, Hoot dusts the dash with his middle finger. Then he smacks the fuzzy blue dice hanging from the rear view mirror and they bounce back and forth.

For the last hour Nick has cracked his knuckles and studied the road map. The map is from triple A and so detailed Marla feels even she could get them to New York with it. But Marla isn't interested in any road map.

She has come on this trip strictly to be with Hoot. Instead she is sitting in the back seat with Betty Sue who has filed her long red nails ever since they left West Virginia. That was seven hours ago.

They have already come through Cleveland and are heading East on I-90. Hoot says Erie is their next stop. Marla is glad. Several hours ago they ate the bologna sandwiches she packed and she is hungry.

She pulls a tortoise-shell mirror from her purse and looks at herself. She pats her face with a tissue to take the shine off. She dabs some Paris Pink on her lips and blows her blond bangs off her forehead. She wishes it wasn't so hot. Hoot has the air-conditioner off. He says it saves on gas. Marla puts the mirror away and turns back to the billboards and signs.

That's how she is keeping busy. Reading billboards and signs. For what seems like hours now they have traveled past vineyards.

"Bob's Winery five miles ahead," Marla reads aloud in a monotone as they pass a billboard featuring a giant glass of bubbling champagne. She brightens, "Oh, let's stop!"

"Bob's Winery! Three miles ahead!"

"One mile!"

They come to the exit for Bob's Winery. Marla's eyes light up. A neon sign is flashing "Bob's Winery Here."

Hoot doesn't even slow the car. If anything, he speeds up. Marla closes her eyes and tries to imagine what a winery would be like. But even trying hard, she can't.

Now she fluctuates between reading signs and staring at the back of Hoot's head. She would love to touch his soft black hair but doesn't. He hates having his hair touched. He carries a comb in his back pocket and won't let one hair get out of place. Marla catches Hoot's eye in the rear view mirror. She smiles but he doesn't let on that he sees her. More and more lately he doesn't let on that he sees her. Sometimes she wonders if she is invisible. One day she was in the IGA and he looked right past her.

Between his long hours at the fire station and his singing gigs they are lucky to be together every other week now. When the idea for the trip came up, Marla was glad. This could be an investment in her future.

Betty Sue is busy highlighting certain passages in a *True Story Magazine* with a lemon-scented marker.

The air is heavy with HaiKarate. Hoot's. Marla loves smelling it on him. Especially when he is beside her on the blue shag carpet of her apartment watching Days of Our Lives. Hoot isn't hot or cold on any of the stars. But, Patch and Kayla are Marla's favorites. They are so much in love it hurts Marla to watch them. Something always happens to keep them apart. Patch is so open with his emotions it makes Marla want to cry. Marla can't imagine Hoot ever acting over her like Patch does over Kayla. Sometimes she wishes she wasn't so crazy in love with Hoot. She isn't so sure his feelings for her are all that deep. Particularly these days. He seems so preoccupied.

Suddenly Hoot slams on the brakes and Marla and Betty Sue are nearly thrown into the front seat. A flat-bed truck has come to a complete stop on the highway in front of them. The driver of the truck is an old man who seems to have missed his exit and is starting to back up toward them.

Without pause, Hoot passes, laying on the horn and giving the old man the finger.

Hoot and Nick get into a big discussion of fishing for bass. Marla knows for a fact all Hoot knows about fishing for bass is what he has read in the *Outdoor Journal of Ohio, Pennsylvania and West Virginia* which he reads from cover to cover. As far as Marla knows Hoot has never been fishing and he lives near the river.

"I want to be a pro at it when I do go," he said to her once when she complained that he should be fishing not reading. He is the only person Marla knows who wants to read about everything. Just the week before he read a dozen books on the Falls.

"Hand me one of them Cokes, Marla," Hoot says now and she takes the lid from the red and white plastic cooler at her feet, opens the can and hands it over the seat. Her older sister, Shirley Jean, says Marla lets Hoot boss her too much. Maybe she does. But she wants to marry Hoot so bad she will do almost anything he asks to please him.

It was the invitation to her class reunion that really got her thinking. She is the only girl from her class who is still single. Her mother laughs and says she's only 23 and why worry. But she does.

She has heard Hoot laugh and say that the life of a firefighter isn't one for a married man. He says the job is too dangerous. But, Marla doesn't buy any of this. If there's any danger it's in Hoot's head.

The Chesterville fire truck hardly ever leaves the station except when Hoot drives it up to the IGA for groceries. That's how she met him. In the express check-out. They'd struck up a conversation over a can of Chefboyardee Ravioli which was on special and exactly what they'd both come there to buy. That was last summer. They have been seeing each other off and on ever since.

Marla is hoping when they get to the Falls they can be alone. That somehow there will be a turning point. Something tells her this trip is more than just a simple trip. She's brought along a bottle of Andre Champagne and two plastic champagne glasses from K-Mart just in case.

At the Falls they plan to get two rooms. She will have to bunk with Betty Sue. But somehow or other she plans to get Hoot alone.

Hoot is interested mainly in the Elvis Presley Museum. Marla doesn't care about seeing a living room lamp from Graceland or the first dollar-bill Elvis ever made. But she would never tell Hoot that. Elvis is more than Hoot's idol. It spooks Marla to think about it. How much Hoot is like Elvis. Down to how he lifts his lip when he sings. Even his mother's name is Grace.

Hoot and Marla's relationship has developed mostly in Marla's apartment on Main Street over top of Charlie's U-Call-We-Haul Trucking Company in the few hours she isn't working the McDonald's drive-thru. That's how she was able to come on this trip. She takes every hour she can get.

Earlier, as they were loading the car for the trip, Marla mentioned riding the Maid of the Mist. And visiting Tussaud's Wax Museum. Charlie, from U-Call, said George Burns looks real and Marla wants to see for herself. Hoot didn't say one way or the other. All he said was he heard you got wet riding the Maid of the Mist. He was in the middle of telling Nick about the Elvis Museum and how they were about to see the largest private collection of Elvis memorabilia in the world. Nick wasn't even listening, just tossing suitcases into the trunk as fast as he could and blowing bubbles with a wad of Juicy Fruit.

In Erie they gas up at a Sunoco and then Hoot parks over to the side of the station and they all go to use the restrooms. On the way back they get ham sandwiches out of a machine and Marla buys herself a Zagnut and gets a Zero for Hoot. He loves Zeros. They are hard to find. She decides to buy two.

Nick stares at Marla as they get back into the car. She is wearing a red halter top with her navy shorts and her new leather sandals. She has the best tan she's ever had. She's been twenty times to the tanning bed. She just hopes she doesn't get skin cancer for being so vain.

Hoot has never noticed that she is evenly tanned all over. She notices everything about him. He only gets a tan on his face and arms. He never wears shorts. She is surprised he will wear muscle shirts. But he does. He has one on now and she loves him in it. It is red to match her halter top. She has asked him specifically to wear the shirt.

In the front seat Hoot and Nick are arguing over the route they are taking. Hoot says he bets there is a more direct route to Buffalo. He said they probably didn't need to go through Cleveland at all. He accused Nick of wanting to go through Cleveland just to say he'd been there. Nick has people in Euclid.

Marla doesn't care which route they take. She just wants to get there.

She has brought enough clothes to stay two weeks but they only plan to be gone for four days. The trunk is packed full and Hoot even has one suitcase tied on top of the Monte Carlo.

Shirley Jean, who used to work for Reynolds Aluminum, has lent Marla all of her clothes. They both wear a size 7. Her mother has said to enjoy being small because the women in her family tend to pick up weight when they have babies. Marla doesn't particularly like babies. She isn't sure she wants any for herself.

"I bet if you marry Hoot and he wants a dozen kids you'll probably jump right in and have 'em," Shirley Jean teased Marla as she folded clothes for the trip. Marla just smiled.

Shirley Jean is dating a man called Eddie from Virginia. He drives over almost every week-end. He has a boat back in Virginia and he has offered to take them all out in it. Hoot can't swim. She thinks this may be why he always turns Eddie down. She can swim and has been begging Hoot to go.

Eddie is the opposite of Hoot. He started getting his tan early at a tanning bed too and now is golden brown. His brown hair is streaked with gold and much of the time he visits Shirley Jean he wears only swimming trunks. He has a 14K gold chain around his neck and wears a nugget ring. Marla has asked Hoot to wear a gold chain but he refuses. She bought him one for Christmas but he took it back and got some flannel shirts with the money.

Betty Sue has been massaging Nick's neck over the seat. Marla is sure they have an intimate relationship just by the way they act when they're together. At least Nick has told Betty Sue he wants to marry her. He has talked about going to Cleveland to look for a job. He is laid-off from his construction job. He is a welder, a good one he says, and can get work anywhere. Hoot says Nick is all talk. Marla wonders.

Hoot pulls into a roadside park. The Monte Carlo is starting to heat up. Betty Sue and Nick disappear laughing into a grove of trees. Hoot appears agitated as he swings out of the car and puts the hood up. He leans against a tree to smoke.

Marla sits in the car for a minute before getting out to lean against the tree with Hoot. She moves over and kisses him. He kisses her back. But for only a minute.

"Hey," he says, looking over his shoulder, "there's people around." She sees one man at the far end of the park. Otherwise they are alone. She puts her arms around Hoot again and he pushes her away, this time Marla loses her balance and nearly falls.

Just then a semi pulls in not far from them and the bearded trucker that gets out looks Marla over from head to toe. He smiles and winks. Hoot has his head under the hood of the car and doesn't see.

The thought that he wouldn't care if he did see makes Marla's breath catch in her throat. It is at that exact moment that she knows for sure what she has suspected all along. Hoot has no intention of riding the Maid of the Mist. Or visiting the Tussaud's Wax Museum. Or marrying her. Not now. Not ever.

A cold wind whips across the parking lot and Marla shivers. She reaches into the back seat for her sweater and notices the brown bag with the champagne. She takes it from the car and heads to the rest room. Inside the cubicle she stares at the Andre Champagne and the two plastic glasses for a moment before pushing them through the lid of the trash can. They hit the metal bottom with a loud clatter.

She unwraps a Zero and eats it as she walks back to the car.

"How far have we got to go?" she asks as Hoot closes the hood of the car.

"Not far," he says. He slides into the car, turns on the ignition and the radio at the same time. "Wasted days and wasted nights," Hoot sings loudly, nearly drowning out Freddy Fender.

Betty Sue and Nick smile as they get into the car.

Nobody notices Marla as they head down the highway. She is ripping the brochure for the Elvis Museum into the tiniest pieces and is letting them blow, one by one, out the window and into the hot air.

Joy Ruth and Minnie Hendrix

Every Wednesday at noon, Joy Ruth takes old Minnie Hendrix to McDonald's. She pushes the wheelchair up to the counter where the old woman orders a Big Mac, large fries, and a black coffee.

Today, they are sitting in the newly remodeled section which has green plastic ferns hanging from the ceiling.

"My tail bone is killing me," Minnie complains as she eats. She has just turned eighty and is a finicky eater. McDonald's is the only place she will finish her food.

"Raise up a minute," Joy Ruth says, "and let's see if we can fix that skinny tail bone of yours." Minnie grasps the wheelchair and raises herself up. The young woman reaches over from the green plastic booth and fluffs the flowered pillow underneath the old woman.

Satisfied, Minnie sinks back into the pillow and straightens her red satin dress.

Every week the old woman insists on wearing the red satin dress with food stains on the bodice. Joy Ruth offers her other outfits but the old woman insists on the satin dress. When her mind is set, it is set. Like the funeral home issue.

"Miller's has some new caskets," Minnie says, eating a handful of fries, "Louella went with the Moose to pick out a casket for that poor boy who drove his car into Lick Creek. His daddy was a Moose." She licked her lips. "Or he was a Moose. Until he shot himself. Now the boy is dead too." She clears her throat. "Louella says they have a payment plan. Or you can pay cash for the whole she-bang. It can't hurt none to go and look." Her eyes plead with Joy Ruth. "Well, can it?"

"Mommy will want to go over to that funeral home, I bet my boots on it." Minnie's middle-aged daughter, Laverne, chain-smoked from a crumpled pack of Kool's and rested her red boots on a ladder back chair across from Joy Ruth. Both women were seated at Minnie's kitchen table. It was Joy Ruth's first day on the job. "Planning her own funeral is an obsession of mommy's, and I'll tell you this," Laverne pursed her lips and blew a smoke ring right at Joy Ruth, "there is no telling mommy no. Not when she gets something in her head."

Joy Ruth had applied for the job just that morning. "Companion and Driver for Elderly Woman Who Has All Her Faculties." After Joy Ruth drove the old woman's '55 Chevy up and down the driveway a number of times, Minnie, seated beside Joy Ruth, said with a grin, "Well, girl, you got yourself a job."

That afternoon when she returned to the house after taking Minnie to her weekly hair appointment, Joy Ruth found Laverne seated in the kitchen.

"Hell will freeze over before I'll take her to pick out stuff she'll wear when she's dead. I told her so too. I don't think I could make myself any clearer." The tall jean-clad woman lit another cigarette. "Mommy will put you up to asking Hollister but don't. Hollister might be her only son but he agrees with me on this one." She blew a line of tiny smoke rings at Joy Ruth. "Picking out burial stuff while you're still living is a sick thing to do." She smashed the long cigarette against the words *"New York"* in the bottom of the ashtray. "We didn't even pick out stuff for daddy."

She stood and shook long dark gray-streaked hair around her shoulders. She started pacing across the kitchen floor. "Mommy was too doped up on Librium to make decisions. The undertaker took care of it.

"Good God," she sighed, "I say we cross that bridge when we come to it." She went to the refrigerator, took the cap off a plastic bottle of Coke and tipped it to her lips. "Good luck is all I can say, Joy Ruth." She wiped her mouth with the back of her hand and returned the bottle to the refrigerator. "You're gonna need it with Mommy."

***

From the window of McDonald's, Joy Ruth and Minnie are watching a big car pile up out in front. "Maybe Laverne will take you over there," Joy Ruth says to Minnie and nods her head in the direction of the funeral home across the street. Joy Ruth knows the old woman's daughter won't take her, yet she can't help adding, "It's Laverne's place."

"Laverne's place!" The old woman sputters and spits out a bite of Big Mac. "When did Laverne ever know her place? Both of my kids together don't make one good kid." She starts chewing on her sandwich again. "I ought to change my will." She reaches for the pickle slice Joy Ruth has taken off her sandwich, and pops it into her painted red mouth. "I might too," she says. She bites into the pickle and makes a face.

"It's sundae time," Joy Ruth announces, hoping to take Minnie's mind off her will. She eases herself out of the booth and gathers their sandwich wrappings.

"I want butterscotch," Minnie calls as the young woman heads to the trash bin. "Tell that smart aleck girl to make mine with real ice cream. I hate imitation. I want real ice cream."

As soon as Joy Ruth gets her home the old woman falls asleep in her rocking chair. Joy Ruth runs water over the dishes in the kitchen sink and stares out the window at the plastic flowers stuck in the window box below.

"They bloom summer and winter," the old woman said proudly the day she interviewed Joy Ruth, "no weeding and no watering." She leaned closer to the window to get a better look at her small yard. "See that white plastic duck out there and that bird bath. Laverne gave them to me." She turned from the window and made a sweeping gesture around her kitchen at the various knickknacks, "Laverne and Hollister both give me things." She picked up a black and white ceramic cow with the lettering "*Niagara Falls*" and dusted it with the hem of her dress. "Only they don't have no time for me."

Now, as Joy Ruth washes dishes, suds from the Ivory Liquid trailing up her arms, she can see that the plastic duck with the bright orange bill has fallen onto its side and the ornately carved bird bath is full of dead leaves and rain water. Right then, she decides, she will take Minnie to the funeral home. Goose bumps cover her arms at the very thought of going over there.

Miller's Funeral Home is never far from Joy Ruth's mind. But it isn't funerals Joy Ruth is interested in. It is Leroy Miller.

Joy Ruth's crush on Leroy has lasted all her life. When he left West Virginia after high school to go to the Cincinnati College of Mortuary Science, she was sure she'd never see him again. When she heard he'd married a girl from there she stopped looking for him back. But he had returned and he returned alone. That was five years ago and in all that time she has never gone near the funeral home.

"Joy Ruth!" the old woman calls, "Joy Ruth!"

The younger woman rushes into the living room, hurriedly wiping her hands on a dancing cow dishcloth as she goes, to find a smiling Minnie Hendrix sitting up, ramrod straight, in her chair, refreshed after her short cat nap and ready to visit.

"Did I ever tell you that Chenille is the only person who is good to me?" Minnie runs her hand across the afghan on her lap. "You know Chenille, Hollister's new wife. All that girl ever does is polish her fingernails. But she kisses me when she comes in and she says, and how are you today, Miss Minnie? She says it every time. It counts for something, I can tell you that. Do you know how many people say, how do you feel today, Minnie?

"Not a one," she answers herself. "They don't ask because they don't want to know. Do you know why they don't want to know?"

Joy Ruth finishes drying her hands and sits down on the sofa. Minnie points her finger at Joy Ruth. "I'll tell you why they don't want to know. If they know, they might have to do something. Like get Miss Minnie a drink. Or hand her a pill. Or go to the grocery store. People don't want to do for their own people anymore." She shifts her weight around in her chair and resumes her rocking. "I raised some smart cookies, I'll say that for myself." She leans back in her chair and closes her eyes. "Put that in your pipe and smoke it, Joy Ruth. And you can tell Laverne every word I said. I know she pumps you every chance she gets. Do you know how I know? I'm not always sleeping when my eyes are closed."

At home later, Joy Ruth makes a grilled cheese sandwich with tomato wedges for her supper. She eats, washes and dries the Teflon skillet, and hangs it on the wall behind the stove just above the shelf that holds her collection of little wooden houses.

She picks up the television remote in the living room and runs through the channels. She stops at the Inspirational Network. Brother Robison is pacing across the television screen wringing his hands. Tears run in two streams down his cheeks. Joy Ruth curls up on the sofa to watch the show.

"Please brothers and sisters," the man says, "open your hearts and your checkbooks," he wipes his eyes with a white handkerchief, "and send your generous love offering to Brother Robison today. Do it now," sweat drips from the heavyset man on the screen in front of Joy Ruth, "check or money order. Makes no difference folks. Whatever is easiest for you." He paces back and forth. "Riches will flow upon your life," he says, "and thank you again from the bottoms of our hearts for keeping this ministry alive." He bows his head in prayer as the credits roll across the screen.

Brother Robison's healing show comes on next. It is a rerun and Joy Ruth's favorite. Right off, Brother Robison heals a crippled Rabbi. The man walks off the stage pushing his own wheelchair. Then the minister puts his hand on the shoulder of a woman who is wearing a gold beaded dress. He asks if she knows she has a tumor. She shakes her head no, her eyes wide with fear. He clasps her shoulder tightly and then lets go. She reels backward and then starts jumping up and down pogo-stick-fashion.

Joy Ruth shivers and draws the quilt from the back of the sofa around her. She can feel Brother Robison's power right there in her own living room. Sometimes she has to reach over and place her hand on the Bible that sits on the table to steady herself. She is convinced Brother Robison is on the up and up. Minnie Hendrix believes in him too. They discuss Brother Robison for hours. Joy Ruth wants to take Minnie to visit Brother Robison. Maybe he can heal the old woman of the rheumatism that causes her legs to be useless at times.

***

"It's a wonder Hollister can't heal me," Minnie says when they watch Brother Robison. "He's the most saved man I know. He gets saved every Sunday. They pray over him to beat the band. That's over to the Church of The Living Spirit. He says he renews his salvation. I guess you can't be too saved. Hollister don't believe in TV preachers. He didn't, that is, until he married Chenille. Her daddy preaches on WDOK."

The next day, Hollister brings Minnie's mail from the post office. Joy Ruth and Minnie are watching Brother Robison. Tears stream down both of their faces. Minnie sits stone-still in her rocker and Joy Ruth perches on the edge of the brown plaid sofa.

"That Robison guy has people right where he wants 'em," Hollister remarks, handing Minnie a Swiss Colony catalog and a statement from Medicare. "In his pocket," he laughs. "Get it? In his pocket!" He lowers himself onto the sofa beside Joy Ruth, his big frame taking up all the available space. "I can't believe people is stupid enough to send that thief money. Love offering my foot."

Minnie's eyes catch Joy Ruth's and Joy Ruth gets the message loud and clear. With Hollister's eyes riveted to the television, the young woman slides the envelope holding their love offering under the worn black Bible on the table.

By the time the gold-robed choir comes on, Hollister is reclining on the sofa, eating a carton of raspberry yogurt from Minnie's hiding place in the back of her refrigerator, his feet resting on Minnie's brown leather hassock.

"Swing low, sweet char-i-ot, com-in' for to carry me home," Minnie's surprisingly strong voice rings out as she sings along with the choir, "swing low, sweet char-i-ot, com-in' for to carry me home."

"I want this sung at my funeral, Hollister," Minnie says, "now listen carefully to these words.

"Swing low, sweet char-i-ot, com-in' for-to-car-ry-me-home.

"Remember that, son." She closes her eyes, and finishes the song with great enthusiasm, "Com-ing-for-to-car-ry-me-home!"

The next Wednesday, Joy Ruth drives the '55 Chevy past McDonald's and parks in front of Miller's. Her knees shake as she wheels Minnie up the handicapped ramp and into the service elevator where Leroy Miller is waiting for the ride up to the Casket Parlor.

"Let me warn you ladies," he says as the elevator door closes, "all you will see is caskets when this door opens. It may take your breath away. It does some folks that way. Now here we go."

They are quickly swooshed upwards. The elevator door pops open and they face a room full of caskets. He leads them through a doorway and into a sitting room that smells faintly of lilacs. Joy Ruth sees a can of Glade room spray on a little table in the corner.

"You'll want to read this over," Leroy Miller says to Minnie and hands her a form. She barely glances at it and hands it back. He motions Joy Ruth to sit down on a gold brocade sofa.

"We worked out most of the details on the phone," he says, "some of that information may change. Like the addresses of your kids. We can update that when the time comes. But we got the important stuff. Would you like a mint?" He hands Minnie a silver candy dish filled with miniature York peppermint patties.

"Well, thank you," she says, scooping up a handful of the mints and hands the dish to Joy Ruth. Without taking any candy, Joy Ruth places the candy dish back on the glass table.

"You better have a couple of those mints," the old woman says to Joy Ruth, "it's hard to tell how long this business will take."

"This business won't take long," Leroy says, briskly. He wears a dark suit and tie. Joy Ruth's eyes almost meet his but she blushes and turns away. She can't bring herself to look at him. She is aching to know if he remembers her. Everyone in school knew she had a crush on him.

"Now if you're ready," he says to Minnie and stands, "we'll go look at those caskets."

"I'm ready as I'll ever be," she says. She unwraps another peppermint pattie and pushes it into her mouth.

Gripping the wheelchair, the man turns the old woman in the direction of the Casket Parlor. "Let's see if we can find something in here you like." He wheels her from one casket to the other, patiently explaining the various features as the old woman peers into each casket and rubs her hand along each satiny interior.

Joy Ruth lingers in the doorway and twists her belt buckle. She notes Leroy's gentleness, and how from time to time, he pats Minnie's frail arm. Her heart pumps faster. She feels warm. It could be the sight of the caskets. Or it could be the closeness of Leroy Miller.

"I want this one right here," Minnie says, wheeling her chair close to Joy Ruth to thump her hand on a gray metal casket. The interior is pale pink.

"Good choice," Leroy says. "It's stainless steel." He walks over and opens a white louver door to reveal a row of chiffon dresses. He pulls out a pink dress and then chooses a lilac one and holds them up for the old woman to inspect. "What do you think?"

"Let me see that one." Minnie points to the pink dress. It comes with a strand of white beads. She takes the dress from Leroy. "This is the one I want. I love pearls." She holds the dress to her, fingers the beads, and turns to Joy Ruth. "How does this one look?"

Joy Ruth smiles and nods. She catches Leroy's eye. He is smiling broadly at her. He remembers.

"Wait until Laverne sees me in this," the old woman chuckles, "I wish I could be there to see her face. She says I don't have good taste. This'll show her who has good taste."

"If that's the one you want, that's the one you'll have," Leroy says, and cheerfully jots down the style number of the pink dress on his yellow pad. He wheels Minnie back into the sitting room where he sits down behind the desk.

Joy Ruth returns to her spot on the gold brocade sofa.

"Write it all up and tell me where to sign," the old woman says and turns to Joy Ruth, "write the man a check, honey."

"Like I said on the phone," he points to some figures on the form, "one fee covers everything."

Minnie squints at the paper he hands her. "I can't make it out."

"Six thousand even. That includes a good steel vault. The service will be here in the chapel. You can decide on a minister and singers. If you want singers. Or your family can decide. That is, when the time comes."

"I already planned the whole she-bang," the old woman looks at him over her glasses as she signs the check. "I wrote out my instructions already. They're in my safe. I got me a Montgomery Ward safe and Hollister knows where I keep the combination. Right under my handkerchiefs in the little vanity drawer. I want Preacher Cobb," she hands Leroy the check, "he's from Hollister's church. I picked some singers. I like good singing, don't you? I picked three groups. That's in case some of them can't make it. Who knows? They may be dead. If so," Minnie starts to laugh, "Laverne can sing. Wouldn't that be a hoot."

"You are doing your loved ones a big favor," Leroy closes the folder on his desk. "Now you go out of here and live 20 more years. You can rest easy knowing everything is fixed the way you want it." He sits back and loosens his tie. "Did I tell you that price includes the hairdo? I was noticing your hair. You have pretty hair. Our woman here is good with hair. We haven't had any complaints, anyway."

Minnie laughs. "That's a good one, now. Yes, sir, that's good!"

"You come on over to McDonald's with us, Leroy," she offers, smoothing the skirt of her red satin dress, "the Big Mac's are on me."

As the three of them move toward the service elevator, Leroy maneuvering the wheelchair, Joy Ruth feels light as air. Like she might fly away. She touches Leroy's arm to ground herself.

Micro Wave

The only time Micro ever left his house was at dusk to walk his pug dog, Dumpling. Neighbors got used to the sight of the old man and the pug, both huffing and puffing with every step, as they made their way down to the old wooden pier, jutting out into the Ohio River. Once there, the two would sit on that old pier until dark or after, catching their breath and gazing out into the dark water.

"Didn't always have breathing problems," Micro said, "but years of chain smoking spotted my lungs. Now old Dumplin' here," he said, "well, he come to me snortin' and snuffin'. No bigger than my hand when I got him." He studied the palms of his big calloused hands and then bent and patted the little dog.

Back when Micro moved into the house on the lower east side, down next to the river, he said his name was Micro Wave. His disability checks came addressed that way so people figured he was telling the truth. Or the truth as far as Micro knew it. Truth to Micro wasn't always truth to the others. Neighbors learned that about the old man right off.

He told stories that made people wonder. Like the one about a wife named Ocean Wave and about being part of the Woodstock scene and the Hough Avenue Riots and the Kent State shootings.

Micro was neither black nor white but somewhere in between. He said he didn't stand for any one race but stood for many. He played Chuck Berry records on his phonograph, original 45's. Not worn. Worth something, he said.

"Oh, Maybelline, why can't you be true, oh, Maybelline, why're you doin' those things you used to do." The music floated out through the open windows of Micro's house, drifting out through long white curtains that billowed onto the porch, wrapping Chuck's words in gauze. Wooden spoons propped in the windows held them open year round.

Dumpling would snore and Chuck would sing. No wonder the old man's hearing was nearly shot. Or so he said, when he was still talking to the neighbors.

On Friday nights, he used to come and sit with the neighbors, whoever had chairs out, and he'd talk until he ran out of words. Or until he'd take a coughing fit. He would start on the weather and how it was changing and go on to Ocean Wave and how with her the tide was always turning.

One of the neighbors would finally stick a finger up to his own ear and draw a circle, indicating to the group that Micro was crazy. Others, though, drew in every word he uttered. He may have been crazy, but he was entertaining-crazy on hot summer nights.

Right before he quit coming out of his house for anything except to walk his pug dog at dusk, he told me in detail how it was at Kent State. The National Guard. The shots ringing out. The blood. And that awful sound of the screaming. How it made his ears ring, even today. He couldn't have told it as well if he hadn't been there.

Some people came away with pictures of it, he said. He came away with a scar. Neighbors never saw any scar. It could be his scar was in a place eyes couldn't see. Maybe not even his own.

Wally and Bun

Wally Hall sold lamps for a living. Not for Sears Roebuck or J.C. Penney's or any store like that. He sold for Mohr's Light House in the Centerville Shopping Plaza.

Wally graduated from high school with Mr. Mohr's only son, Murphy. Not that Wally was in Murphy's league.

The only thing Wally'd ever had in common with Murphy Mohr was Nadine. Murphy had taken Nadine, who was a flag girl and looked terrific in short skirts, to the Senior Prom. But it was Wally who married her. Wally and Nadine weren't still married or anything like that. All told, the marriage lasted less than three months. Longer than Wally gave it under the circumstances.

Nadine'd missed a period, the one right after Prom. And with Murphy Mohr's career ahead of him, Nadine eventually explained it all to Wally---how Murphy had already been accepted at Harvard and said he'd never sell a lamp in his lifetime---Nadine threw herself on Wally (they were working the line at Wendy's) and sobbed her eyes out. What could Wally do?

Ever since Wally could remember, Nadine Hakes had been there. Seated in front of him every school year. Her locker next to his at Dunlap High. Her picture flanking his in the yearbook. It had always been that way. Nadine Hakes and Wally Hall. On graduation day, he'd stood so close behind her, he had tripped on the back of her white gown and knocked over a folding chair.

As soon as Nadine found out that nothing was on the way, she had split. Oh, Wally hadn't expected her to stay. And, he hadn't had a girl since. Well, he hadn't actually had Nadine. During their brief marriage, she'd slept in his maple bed and he'd slept on the living room couch. He'd moved Nadine in with her set of Samsonite luggage, a graduation gift from her parents and her Flag-Girl-of-the-Year trophy.

That was ten years ago. Enough time had passed to give Wally a chance to grow into himself. And he liked who he was.

Now Wally dressed for the public. He went for a casual but expensive look. He wore Dingo snakes which he'd bought at the Bootery for $165 and an imitation snake belt to match. He always wore black slacks. With 7 pairs he had to go to the coin laundry only once a week. And he favored white silk shirts.

Wally wasn't sure what it was about his job that he liked so well. The money was inadequate and he worked long hours without compensation. Mr. Mohr himself wasn't too bad a guy. He was short and squat and chewed a stubby cigar. He was generous at Christmas with a cash bonus and he always threw in a Butterball turkey, a 15-pounder, which his mother, Juanita, cooked and Wally carried home in a Ziploc bag Christmas evening.

It was the store that brought Wally Hall his greatest joy. Mr. Mohr had fine furniture and paintings to show off all the wonderful lamps. Wally and Mr. Mohr fussed over the showrooms, flicking dust off a table here and straightening a painting there. With all the lamps lit the store was a glittering bright arena where Wally spent his happiest hours.

He carried a large, smart looking leather attache case with two combination locks. Inside it, he kept all his valuables, the will he had made after his trip to the emergency room in the squad car, his life insurance policy naming Juanita beneficiary, and the deed to one lot in Memory Gardens which Juanita had given him for his 18th birthday. Then, there was the bag of Smarties tucked in one corner. Wally craved the little candies but he only ate them when no one was around.

Wally's brother, Burt, was a tree man. He called himself a tree surgeon. What he did was go around spraying trees and bushes with various kinds of high-powered sprays which Wally was sure would eventually cause Burt to have skin cancer or some lung disorder.

Burt didn't have a drop of Wally's sensitivity or taste for anything other than what he had. He had quit school in the 11th grade and then gone back and got his GED, whereas Wally had gone to the local college off and on since high school. While he didn't have enough credits for a degree, he'd taken everything from ballet to a course in pharmacology, he had a broad spectrum of things he could discuss. Not that he spent much time in conversation with his customers at Mohr's.

Wally's most important customer was Maybelle Stout, wife of the late Mayor Will E. Stout, who'd made his money in Burger Kings. Will E. had bought in on the ground floor. Unfortunately, he had a heart attack and dropped dead, all 300 pounds of him, one day while standing in line at the new store near Flattop. Maybelle said burgers had taken Will E. up and brought him down.

Maybelle sought Wally's lighting expertise as she redecorated the stately old mansion that sat high on a hill overlooking the Shenandoah Park River. Will E. had bought it from Barnaby Skraggs, owner of Shenandoah Downs Race Track. The motif throughout the house was horses. Wallpaper in the living room. Murals in the study. Mirror tiles in the shape of horses racing along the hallways. With Will E. gone, Maybelle had given herself over to the project of removing the horses. She came into the store, her arms filled with carpet samples, swatches of wallpaper and paint samples.

"Butterflies," she gushed at Wally, "I'm going into butterflies." She crowded her sentences with words such as dainty and delicate. Wally ran back and forth between the lamps and chandeliers jotting down style numbers while she talked on and made animated gestures with her hands causing the long gold butterflies dangling from her ears to spin in circles. All Wally was interested in was getting the stuff ordered and delivered on time. Maybelle's ambition was to have a chandelier with a thousand crystal butterflies lighting the main dining hall.

Wally's sister-in-law, Rita, was another butterfly nut. She had butterflies everywhere, even one made out of a coat hanger on the front door of their double-wide. She'd made Wally a throw pillow with a needlepoint butterfly on it for Christmas and for his birthday she gave him a toilet tissue cover with plastic butterflies circling the rim.

When Rita wasn't making Wally a butterfly gift she was trying to fix him up with someone. Her latest attempt was her sister, Trish.

Trish had just had a nose job. The night Wally took her to the movie to see The Fly II he told her, "Your new nose is real cute." He told her that even though her nose was swollen and black and blue. When Wally held her hand during a scary part, Trish whispered, "Men who are balding turn me on."

Later, Wally heard Trish tell Rita out in the kitchen that she thought he was funny looking and he had sweaty palms. They were having pizza with anchovies, Trish's pick, and Wally was half sick.

That was the night Wally thought he was dying. He had ridden in the emergency squad, siren screaming, to find out he was having a major attack all right. Of indigestion not heart. Wally was glad when Trish went back to Albany. That's where Burt met Rita. She was waiting tables in a truck stop on the New York freeway and Burt was driving for Yellow. He was only on the road two months when he had an accident. It was minor but his nerves wouldn't let him go back. That's when he went into trees and married the butterfly nut.

As for Murphy Mohr, he had become an attorney, married his college sweetheart, and "located down south." "Yes," Mr. Mohr would say expansively, working the cigar around in his mouth, as he feather-dusted this lamp or that, "The boy has located down south." He worked this into conversation as often as he could.

Wally's path never once crossed Murphy Mohr's as far as Wally knew. Murphy and his wife came back to town only once and that was for his mother's funeral. It was in News and Notes in the Record. "Murphy and Ashley Mohr of Mohr & Mohr of Asheville, North Carolina," it said, "were in town to attend the funeral of Murphy's dearly beloved mother."

Not long afterward, Mr. Mohr met and married Ginger Lee. Her stage name. Wally finally figured it out. She was a dancer. Mr. Mohr was always quick to add, "former."

Wally heard Murphy Mohr was unhappy with his father's marriage. But Wally appreciated the constant smile on Mr. Mohr's face and the spring in his step.

Ginger Lee stopped by the store every day at noon to take Mr. Mohr to lunch. He'd bought her a silver Corvette and she acted like she was sixteen in it, honking the horn and waving the minute she pulled up in front of the store. Mr. Mohr was always standing in the window waiting for her.

At first, Wally thought Ginger Lee had her eye on him, the way she stared but he found out pretty quick why she stared. She had a cousin. Now Wally hated cousins. They always ended up being fat, skinny, or ugly. But Ginger Lee's cousin turned out to be Bunny Sue.

She was a dancer too. She asked Wally to call her Bun from the start and he said he would if she'd call him Wal. He hated the name Wally. It was on his birth certificate. Wally Clarence. He'd always hated it. So Wal and Bun it was and for a while Wal was in 7th heaven.

They double dated with Mr. Mohr and Ginger Lee. Mr. Mohr always treated them to dinner at the Coconut Lounge. Now that downtown had been renovated, the Coconut Lounge, formerly The Blue Collar, was the place to go. Wal always ordered Roast Pork with Pineapple Sauce and Bun always ordered Chicken Hawaiian-Style. The waitresses were Oriental and wore grass skirts.

All this put Wal in a Hawaiian mood and he went to the library and checked out a bunch of Don Ho records which he and Bun danced to in his living room. They loved "Tiny Bubbles." All this Hawaiian stuff must have had the same effect on Mr. Mohr and Ginger Lee because the first thing Wally knew they were on a flight to Hawaii.

Wal and Bun saw Mr. Mohr and Ginger Lee off. Mr. Mohr looked great in a red flowered shirt, chewing on his cigar. He'd bought Ginger Lee a lei made of gardenias which made her jump up and down and clap over. The skinny kid from Flo's Florist came into the airport and right up to the United gate and put the flowers around her neck. Wal and Bun were planning to wish the happy couple bon voyage with a box of Russell Stover's chocolates and a bottle of Asti Spumante, but had polished them both off the night before while listening to Don Ho.

Mohr's Light House was empty without Mr. Mohr's boisterous voice. It took a few days for Wal to begin to feel at home as proprietor of

Mohr's. Just like Mr. Mohr had asked him to be. It was then he started making the changes. One or two things a day until the whole store took on a different air.

The first thing to go was Bach and Mozart. Wal turned the piped in music to Cheap Trick and Motley Crue and Def Leppard. This was mainly Bun's idea. She'd never warmed up to Bach, she said.

The new music seemed to pulsate inside Wal until his feet fairly danced across the new floor. Up had come the plush carpet and down had gone white inlaid. Bun had purchased dozens of wind chimes at an outdoor auction and hung them from the ceiling. The slightest movement sent a melodious chiming throughout the store. It gave Wal a heady feeling. Bun said it was the incense.

Wal had a strobe light installed in the main showroom. Reflecting off the mirrors, the light gave the room an unreal feel.

Bun helped Wal re-arrange the showrooms, moving the more traditional Stiffels to the back and bringing out every odd lamp Mr. Mohr had collected over the years.

Wal started wearing his shirts open at the neck to show off the gold chain Bun gave him. It was for their two month anniversary. She bought him turquoise and purple shirts with socks to match and a bottle of Polo which made her melt, she said. He bought Bun a gigantic box of turtles and a big yellow bunny which she named Bunny Too and propped on Wal's desk at Mohr's to remind him of her. Excitement rode high every day that first week with changes being made every minute.

The second week, two things happened. Murphy Mohr came back to town, his marriage to Ashley, "in ashes," he said. And Mohr & Mohr law firm was no more. Maybe he'd sell lamps after all, he told Wal over coffee at Dickie's Donuts next door to Mohr's in the Centerville Shopping Plaza. He wasn't the least bit pleased to learn that Mr. Mohr and Ginger Lee were at the Sheraton on Maui. His eyes nearly fell out of his head at sight of the store.

Then, Nadine came back to town bringing with her a ten-year old kid she called Junior and a demo tape which she was taking to

Nashville. "My sound," she said, tugging at her black leather hot pants, "is similar to the Judd's." She said that when she was interviewed on Beanie's Noon Time News. Bun, who was a Beanie fan, described it all to Wally. It certainly sounded to Wally like Nadine hadn't changed. Except for the red hair. She used to be a strawberry blond.

Murphy Mohr thought she had potential. He caught her at 2 a.m. He almost dropped his corn dog when he saw Nadine staring at him from the television in his den.

"This ain't me you see," she belted into the mike, jerking Murphy wide awake.

"While that squint-eyed little fruitcake Beanie Barker looked on," Murphy complained to Wal late one night. Beanie had graduated as Valedictorian of their class, beating Murphy out by one point."She's a songwriter, too," Murphy added in amazement.

Murphy had taken to calling Wal in the middle of the night and telling him what was on his mind. This kid of Nadine's had him thinking. It had him thinking so much he was planning to call Nadine. Wal asked Murphy to put it on hold until they could discuss it the next day over donuts at Dickie's. This middle of the night stuff was getting to Wal. He could barely keep his eyes open during work hours.

Then, a third thing happened. Mr. Mohr and Ginger Lee bought a place on Maui. They were closing Mohr's Light House in the Centerville Shopping Plaza. They called Wal long distance to say they were selling the business and the house on Beaumont Drive with its white pillars and winding staircase. Not to mention the mirror tiles over the bed in the master suite. Those Wal could see in his mind's eye. Described for him by Nadine the night she'd cried her eyes out on his shoulder at Wendy's. She'd spent her prom night there with Murphy Mohr.

Wal felt the rug being jerked out from under him. He felt like someone caught halfway across a railroad track, looking at an oncoming train. Jump, run, or stand still. None of his choices seemed appealing. For the first time in his life, he was without direction. He didn't know which way was up. He screamed. He cried. He jumped up and down.

He even beat his head on the wall. Right in his own living room with Don Ho singing, "Tiny Bubbles." It didn't change a thing.

Wal found himself unloading on Murphy Mohr during one of Murphy's nocturnal calls. Damn it, anyway, he told Murphy, he was mad. The last ten years of his life had moved forward at a steady pace. Now this. He didn't have the slightest notion what to do. He was a man caught in the middle of a black cloud. With no way out.

Murphy wasn't listening. He was telling Wal for the umpteenth time how Ashley wanted a baby. How she blamed her inability to conceive on his low sperm count. And how he was sure those sperm tests didn't work. They hadn't on him. He was sure of it.

He would talk to Nadine, he said. He was sure that boy was his. Whether Nadine's boy was his or not he already felt like a father. He fell for the kid the minute Nadine produced his school picture on the air. He was any kid U.S.A. Sandy hair. Blue eyes. A winning smile. Murphy was sure beyond the shadow of a doubt the kid was his. Didn't they both have blue eyes? He refused to look at it any other way. Nadine would marry him. He knew she would. He would be the kid's father. And the kid would love him. If Nadine wouldn't marry him, he'd help with the kid. He had some money. He could open a practice right here in the Centerville Shopping Plaza. He'd even sell lamps if he had to. He'd take the kid places. To the zoo. To see the horses run. Murphy spent all his Saturdays at Shenandoah Downs betting on long shots and he knew the kid would love it too. He would talk to Nadine. He told all this to Wal. But Wal, without even saying good-bye, had hung up.

The idea to buy Mohr's Light House in the Centerville Shopping Plaza came to Wal as Murphy Mohr rambled on about his sperm count. Wal felt this great burst of energy welling up inside him---almost as if his own sperm had swelled and burst inside him---until he thought the phone would fly out of his hand. The minute the connection was broken he knew what he had to do. It was so natural he couldn't believe he hadn't thought of it from the start. He'd buy the store from Mr. Mohr. He would be the new owner. He placed a call to Mr. Mohr right then. And before another day dawned, the deal was done.

Bun was beside herself with joy. Before the next day was over she had ordered imported teas and special blend coffees and Country Morning Potpourri in every scent. Wal and Bun's Boutique replaced Mohr's Light House in the Centerville Shopping Plaza.

For a week Wal and Bun hardly left the store. Everything that reminded Wally of Mohr's was gone. The new store had an earthy feel, not at all like the elegance of Mohr's but not at all unpleasant. Being in charge was in Wal's blood. He knew it now and every time he thought of it he got a head rush. During one of his head rushes, this was the only way Wal could figure it, he purchased a pair of tropical birds that were now perched in a large gilded cage in the center of the store.

To Wal's delight a vendor installed candy machines in the entrance of the new store and right there between the M & M's and gum balls was a Smartie machine. Every time Wal passed he put in a dime and got a handful.

"The wedding of Miss Bunny Sue Brown and Mr. Wally Clarence Hall, owners of Wal and Bun's Boutique, took place Saturday on the lawn of the Shenandoah Park Estate, hosted by Maybelle Stout, wife of the late Mayor Will E. Stout." The story was splashed over one full page of the Record. "The couple exchanged vows in the gazebo amid blooming pink roses. The bride wore a white satin gown, it's long train aglitter with sequined butterflies. The groom wore a black tuxedo." The photographer caught Bunny Sue and Wally as they cut the cake. From the lace covered tables at pool side to the rose-petal strewn walkways, the wedding was one the town would long remember. Among the distinguished guests was the new mayor of Centerville, Cheryl Mayne-Mann, who won Maybelle's heart by being photographed beneath the butterfly chandelier.

"After sharing wedding cake and pink champagne, the bride and groom made a grand exit in a hot air balloon which floated off into the blue sky amid cheers and toasts and a shower of pink heart-shaped balloons."

As for Murphy Mohr, he had to drink several glasses of the champagne and loosen his black tie before he could work up enough courage to approach Nadine. She stood alone at the far end of the terrace, her beautiful red hair covering her backless black dress. He asked her to dance. And, they danced and danced. Finally, Murphy Mohr danced Nadine out into the shadows and said all the things he had been wanting to say since that prom night so long ago. He didn't hold back one thing.

As he held her tight in his arms, Murphy Mohr knew beyond the shadow of a doubt there was not a thing wrong with his sperm count. Nadine's warm embrace let him know she knew it too.

Wally Hall looked down from the hot air balloon, the people below him mere dots on the terrain. He smiled and put his hand in Bun's. He was floating in new territory. His heart swelled and lifted with the balloon.

Eve and Marcus Welby

To make her mother think she was actively pursuing a husband, Eve Kelly took courses. Oh, not courses that she was interested in (though for a time she'd liked food service until they'd stopped serving each other) and certainly not courses that would further her career. Eve hadn't been interested in anything except food since Brad had taken his tabby cat, Marcus Welby, and moved out of her apartment and her life. And nothing short of a miracle would move her career in the shipping department of the run-down garment factory where the elderly J.D. Ramsey ruled with a tight fist and a closed mind.

No. Every semester Eve took courses because they were paid for by her mother and presented as a gift for whatever holiday happened to be at hand at the time. May Matheson, presently entertaining her fourth husband, had tired of explaining her 25-year old daughter's unmarried state. With the help of Hilda, her old friend who worked in the admissions office at Community College, May chose courses that had the highest male enrollment. Most of the courses were for credit, though last term Eve had spent six weeks in an adult education class with three giggling girls whose reasons were as undefined as hers, and 15 men, most of them retired and bused to the college, to learn conversational Russian.

If a large percentage of the male population at Community would adhere to a particular field of study, Eve might earn a degree. Nothing else was happening in her life, nothing except her growing dislike for cats and men and her ever-increasing love for food.

The day Brad left, she had rolled into a tight ball on the sofa bed, ready to die. After 24 hours, she got up and moved cautiously through the small apartment. She discovered that while she didn't hurt inside anymore, her ability to feel physical pain was also gone. When opening the few remaining cans of cat food and dumping the contents down the kitchen disposal, she'd cut her finger and didn't know until the blood was spattered all over the sink. As she threw the bloody can into the trash with the others and bandaged her finger, she wondered why she hadn't tossed the food out unopened.

Satisfied that she was cured of cats and men, she went back to work and back to eating and found that the very sight of food could excite her as much as Brad had done on that first day he'd moved in with a bedraggled Marcus Welby hanging over one arm and a bag of dirty underwear over the other. It wasn't long before Brad complained that she stifled his creativity. He painted ceramic figurines for a craft shop and he required space and solitude. Now he was gone, across town to a ceramic buff who had two huge, plastic palm trees in her front window and a valuable collection of china kittens sitting on the dresser in her spare bedroom. So food became Eve's salvation.

The first Monday after Brad left, Eve took a karate lesson. It wasn't a real decision on her part. She was between courses at the college and had tagged along with a group of employees from the garment factory. On the mat, she sat Indian style between two women who were twice her size (though if Eve continued eating she would soon outweigh them both) and practiced breathing. Eve didn't like engaging in physical exercise, especially precise, fast movements, but she watched with a certain amount of enthusiasm as the taut, Oriental instructor took the others through the paces. Suddenly, their graceful movements painfully reminded her of Marcus Welby when he'd leapt from the kitchen counter to the gingham-covered table every morning. With a sob, she fled the class, leaving her co-workers gasping, and vowed never again to think about cats - or men.

All that week at the garment factory she took inventory. J. D. Ramsey refused to hire extra help and while her own work went undone, Eve counted slacks. By the time 3,000 pairs, all burgundy polyester, had passed through her hands, her mouth was dry and her eyes smarted. All she'd ever wanted out of life was a man and a cat. Now she had neither and was determined to survive without both.

On Friday before her first class of the new semester, Eve treated herself to a deluxe shrimp dinner and a hot fudge sundae at a fast food restaurant. By the time she pulled into the campus parking lot, the zipper of her navy blue pants, an outdated style and last year's Christmas gift from J. D., was threatening to give. She hurriedly secured it with the large safety pin she always carried for emergencies and ran up the two flights of stairs to class.

The small class was filled. She counted 11 men and 6 women. Eve took a seat in the back of the room and analyzed the group. All the classrooms were beginning to look alike. The people even resembled the ones she'd left in conversational Russian. But Eve was prepared to make the best of it until the door swung open and the instructor walked in. He was tall, lean and wore a black pullover with a large tabby cat emblazoned on the front. Immediately, she hated him and his iridescent, gold cat.

Opening her interpersonal communications book, Eve scanned the first chapter and remembered May's violent reaction the last time she had dropped a class. But she could deal with May easier than she could sit there for 10 weeks and stare at that cat. The cat was all she'd ever see even if the man wore a suit and a tie.

In a smooth voice, the instructor was naming the various forms of communication. "You communicate something," he said softly, his eyes moving steadily around the room, "by the very clothes you wear." Eve was acutely aware of the large safety pin hidden by her loose shirt. As the man moved effortlessly down each row, passing out exercises and giving reading assignments, she was reminded of a sleek, well-groomed cat.

Later, curled on the sofa bed in semi-darkness, she looked at the outward clutter her life had become: stacks of dirty dishes, piles of rumpled clothes, dust, dead plants. She pulled her muscles tight and studied her body, gazing down at her once spindly legs. Fat sausage toes peeked at her from the bottom of the afghan. And all her life she'd prided herself for landing on her feet.

Until Brad and Marcus Welby had come, she'd been all right. Not perfect but better than average, she'd always joked. She let the past float before her. Brad was short, thin, boyish, but a conquerer, nonetheless. All that wintery day, she'd been out searching for Sammy, her beloved cat who'd escaped her apartment and disappeared in the storm the night before. In a snow-covered parking lot, Brad's old Buick had skidded into the rear end of her new-used Dodge, damaging her "Cat Lovers Are Beautiful People" bumper sticker. Seeing the torn sticker, she'd burst into tears and told Brad, then the sympathetic listener, about Sammy who was blind and had no sense of direction. Right then, Brad had used Marcus Welby to lure her, had used the little gray tabby who'd peered inquisitively at Eve through the frosted car window, as a ploy to get under her roof. Now he was gone. The rationale of it was too sane. Eve had two rooms. The other girl had four, with room for the expansion of Brad's creativity.

Tears began to pour down Eve's face to her chin, spattering onto the cushions of the sofa bed. The pain, when it hit, was brutal. Deep inside, a throbbing, uncontrollable searing worked itself to the surface until her emotional and physical suffering were one. Even the deep cut on her finger burned. As perspiration drenched her body, Eve shook with an icy chill. For the first time in months, she made herself feel until she was saturated, spent.

At dawn, Eve arose and forced herself to go through the apartment, ruthlessly, throwing out everything that wasn't essential to the present. She scrubbed and cleaned and straightened until noon when she stopped for toast and tea and found the insatiable hunger was gone.

The very next week she quit her job at the garment factory and went to work at the humane society wearing her last new pair of J. D. Ramsey's out-of-style slacks. The abandoned tabbies and the little Siamese didn't care. She mixed their food with milk and affection and greedily lapped up their attention.

On Friday night she was late for class. After work she'd shopped for a new pillow and had rearranged the living room to accommodate the kitten's bed. She'd adopted the little Siamese. When she dashed into class she was still wearing the new jeans she'd bought and the shirt she'd made for work. "Cat Lover" was stitched in red across the front.

The instructor's look of annoyance turned to one of interest as Eve took a seat at the front of the room. Her attention was caught instantly and held by the discussion in progress. At the blackboard a student had written in bold print: Barriers To Open Communication. Without hesitating, Eve raised her hand. At the instructor's nod, Eve said firmly, "Fear of rejection."

After class, Eve stopped in the rest room and then walked down the deserted corridor, pausing to stare out one of the large windows overlooking the campus. Outside, fall had come to an abrupt end. A cold, bitter wind was whipping a newspaper to shreds in the parking lot below. A long line of headlights snaked its way toward the open highway.

Sensing she was no longer alone, Eve whirled around to see the instructor standing at the next window. With his arms stretched wide, hands resting on the window frame, he appeared ready to embrace the somber world outside.

"Shall we toast the beginning of winter?" he asked gently, glancing over at Eve.

"Well," she said, hesitantly, as he turned toward the coffee machine against the far wall. Watching him feed coins into the machine, she laughed. "Sure. Why not?"

There, stitched in gold across the man's back, were the glorious words "Cat Lovers Are the Best Kind."

Charlene and Darlene

"I dreamed I had breast cancer and they removed my breast. My left one. They left this big gaping hole." For emphasis Darlene shows me, using her hand to make a scooping motion.

"And then," she goes, "I dreamed you bought this big wooden drapery rod and was trying to use it for those shirr-on-the-rod curtains you bought at the dollar store for your kitchen window."

Darlene is off and running. Her dreams can run on for half a day. I tune out and think my own thoughts. If I didn't, I'd go mad.

I am Charlene. Darlene is my sister. My twin to be exact. People don't believe it. We're that different. Oh, we both have blond hair. But all similarity stops there. Darlene is built to last. She has these long arms and legs that are always in motion. She wishes for all the world to be petite and dainty. Not that I am. I am just more on the average side. It's for this reason, I suppose, that she wears little satin bows in her hair, pinning them right smack on top of her generous head.

Darlene is married to Wayne Johnson who has been in bed for the past two years with arthritis. He's never contributed much in the way of support to her. When he did work he didn't support her. Not in the way you think of supporting someone. Not a roof over her head or food on her table. His money, when he had any --- he worked only sporadically cleaning buses at Trailways --- went to buy Krystle perfume for his mother, Starla, who expired recently choking on a piece of meat in a Big Boy. If you ask me, Wayne and Starla had one of them funny relationships.

It was right after Starla died that Wayne gave Darlene a bus trip to Florida for her birthday, the first time he ever gave her a gift. And lo and behold, she jumped on a bus that very day and rode eighteen hours to see tropical birds, some palm trees, and a dolphin who did a few back flips. The woman's a nut case if you ask me. Never been out of

West Virginia before. Nor since. I too have been out of state only once. I went to Columbus, Ohio to the J. C. Penney Outlet Store. I do not care to go again.

Myself, I would've cashed in that bus ticket and bought something I needed. Like a bed. Which Darlene don't have. She sleeps on her living room couch which doesn't even make into a bed. Now her couch is wore out from her sleeping on it. Stuffing pokes through holes in the cushions. Meanwhile, back in the bedroom that long-haired weasel of a man, Wayne, is in a full-size bed he moved over from his mother's place. He can't stand anybody in bed with him, he says. Darlene, fool that she is, sleeps on her ruined sofa which once was a pretty beige thing with blue peacocks marching across it.

Darlene sees things, too. Things such as Liberace and his piano in the wood grain of her front door.

"Darlene," I said, as she rolled my hair on tiny white rods, "you've got to get a hold on yourself."

"Well, I did see them," she said, dabbing solution on my head with a cotton ball, "dozens of them little poodles racing across my living room floor. Right there." She pointed to the sculptured carpeting. I sat on the floor and she sat behind me on the sofa, giving me my summer perm.

"Honey, you see all this stuff because you don't get rest," I said. "Sleeping on the living room sofa will do that to you. The way the street light shines in, it's no wonder. Besides, you have too much time to lay there alone and think."

That is my opinion. I have learned from Darlene that my opinions and fifty cents will get me a cup of coffee down at the Blue Bell Cafe on Main. Not a very fresh cup either.

About me. I'm the most average person you'd ever want to meet. Nothing at all sets me apart from the crowd. Unless it's my long blond hair which I tease as much as I can to make it stand out around my head like a halo. The Bible says a woman's hair is her glory. In King James it says in 1 Corinthians 15, "But if a woman have long hair, it is a glory to her: for her hair is given her for a covering." Now, that is not to say my hair would cover me entirely but it would cover the most important parts of me. And while I have never covered myself with it except in the privacy of my own bedroom, I believe, if the need ever arose for it to cover me elsewhere, like in a wind storm if my clothes suddenly blew off, it would do so sufficiently.

Something was revealed to me that day as I sat there with the Holy Bible on my lap. I believe I received a divine message from God. My eyes were pulled by a power beyond myself straight up to 1 Corinthians 14, "Doth not even nature itself teach you, that, if a man have long hair, it is a shame unto him?" Now, when the time presents itself, I must bear the burden of revealing this truth to Darlene so that she might reveal it to her no good husband.

Darlene, by the way, was named after our maternal grandmother. My name came from the paternal side. And, speaking of names, our absentee mother, Darnell, should have been named Jezebel, more on this later, or some other more appropriate name for running off and leaving us with our no good daddy.

Now, more about me. I am more religious than Darlene. Going to the Pentecostal Church like I did and playing the tambourine all the years I was growing up---the cinder block church was on the lot next door to where we lived in a trailer---I guess had its influence on me. I am meek as a lamb. Darlene is not. She, in her short shorts and halter top, was laying in the back bedroom of our trailer next door reading *True Romance.*

Growing up, I got enough of house trailers. Now, I live in a real house that's all paid for. The day I graduated from high school (Darlene quit in tenth grade to run off to Flathead, Virginia, and marry Wayne), the car in which I was riding along with five other girls, was hit in the rear by some withered old man in a yellow Cadillac. He used to be president of some bank up in Greenbrier County. He was senile, so his family later said, and shouldn't have been out driving to the Dari-Boy to get a chili dog anyway, and they gave us all, every girl in that Monza, a check for $20,000.

Of course, they said they didn't expect any of us to sue, which we wouldn't have anyway because none of us was hurt. Not really. Dr. Hoak put me in a neck brace for a few weeks. It wasn't a month later, I invested every penny of my money in the house. That was eight years ago.

My house is nice. Not nice as a house out in, say, Knollwood Estates. Those brick homes all have two baths and a family room with a wood burning fireplace. Mine is nice as in modest and unpretentious. It's not a place I'll ever need an alarm system for. Standing in the middle of the house, I can see nearly every window in the place. It's got a fresh coat of white paint outside which I put on myself last summer. I put up the green shutters too, and installed the front porch swing which I got at the church rummage sale. The house has got two tiny bedrooms, a living room big enough to hold my blue velvet love seat which I have never to this day sat on much less slept on, one arm chair, and a portable TV. It has an added-on bath at the back of the house next to the kitchen which is the room I use the most. Not that I cook much. I sit there mostly in the little leatherette booth I had installed by Sears Roebuck and Company and I drink tea and read.

I am a voracious reader. Here Darlene and I split paths. She hasn't read a thing since her *True Romance* days. Not even a recipe card. I read the recipe for her and she mixes ingredients. Me, I read everything I can get my hands on. I have read nearly everything the local library has and they now get me books from all over the state. I never know when I request a book where it will come from. Books have come from places with names such as Redjacket, Peewee, Man, and Lovely. I wonder about the people in Redjacket or Peewee who've read the book before me. What kind of people they are. If they are married or single. Young or old. Rich or poor. If they read in the kitchen as I do hunched over a bowl of Cheerios or Puffed Wheat. Or if they read the book in some fancy room like I've seen in Better Homes and Gardens, maybe a glassed-in room with floor to ceiling plants, overlooking a snowy mountainside such as Canaan Valley. I wonder too what the people in Man or Lovely think about each of the books, say *Morgan's Passing* by

Anne Tyler. I wonder if they think like I do that Morgan is alive and well and will turn up somewhere in my own life. Or do they think he will stay put forever in Tyler's book. No. I hope the people in Man or Lovely think the way I do. That I am different because of Morgan. That he has touched my life. Their life. Our life. That we are all in some way connected because of him.

Currently, I am in a mystery phase and am reading books by Sue Grafton and Mary Higgins Clark. I am glad I am out of the phase where I was reading nothing but books about mother-daughter relationships. One can OD on that stuff. And they are not one ounce helpful.

Besides, my own mother, was somewhere else during the mothering/parenting stage. Even Darlene, who upholds her on everything else, will admit to that one shortcoming. However, it was Darlene who followed in Darnell's footsteps and went to beauty school. Not me. I went into banking. I work the window at First Chemical Savings and Loan.

Now that Darnell is back, Darlene is acting like the woman is a saint. Even doing her hair and nails. Throw-up. It was Darnell who walked off with that long-haired hippie. Not that I recall seeing Darnell's hippie. I recall our daddy, Dallas, calling him, "that dirty long-haired hippie of Darnell's," more times than once. Me and Darlene were ten or eleven. When her hippie went off with someone else, Darnell called and offered to come home to us. But a year had passed and Dallas had taken up with the woman who cleaned the church. "Sorry but nope," he told Darnell on the phone, "I don't need your services any longer."

Darnell came back into our lives anyway one summer afternoon when we were all grown up and least expected it. It was on a Saturday at a family reunion in Krodel Park near Point Pleasant. We were all gathered down by the lake roasting hot dogs and marshmallows.

"My God, Charlene, look who's here," Darlene hissed at me and I nearly dropped my hot dog into the fire. There she was, our mother, traipsing gaily toward us. I'd been standing over that stupid fire for what seemed like forever cooking that hot dog on a stick, letting it get good and done on the inside the way I like it and slightly brown and crisp on the outside. My hair was hanging down in my face, this was before I learned how to tease properly, and I was flushed.

Darnell looked good, made up heavy as ever. There was a new hard look about her though. She was wearing a short purple jumpsuit with large dangling purple ear rings and purple beads strung twice around her neck. Her eyelids glowed purple. She wore silver shoes with little silver bells on the toes that tinkled when she walked. Or tripped. Darnell never walked. She tripped. I will never forget that day as long as I live. No matter if I live to be 100.

"Hell's fire, if it ain't Darnell in the flesh," Uncle Earl called out and grabbed her into a hug like he was some one-man welcoming committee.

Well, I stayed to the outside of the group and didn't linger any longer than it took to eat that one hot dog.

Darlene cozied up to Darnell the minute my back was turned and then came back to me with all these sob stories.

"Get to know her grandkids crap," I said, when Darlene told me that one. I put a book mark into my book to save my place. "She didn't get to know her own kids. Why would she want to know any grandkids? That's what I want to know. Not that I have any for her to get to know. If you're smart you'll keep your girls away from her." Now that she has two girls of her own to raise Darlene feels superior. Her having children even raised Wayne from his bed and got him working, even if halfheartedly, back at Trailways.

"It's sort of like Jesus raising the dead and making the lame walk," I remarked to Darlene, the first time I spotted the miracle of Wayne upright, dressed in jeans and a clean undershirt.

"Charlene," she said, "you are about the most jealous thing. Jealous over my babies, jealous over Wayne and his healing of arthritis, and sometimes I think you are even jealous of our own mama."

"Let me tell you one thing, sister," I said, wanting to make a few things clear anyway, "The last thing I am is jealous over anything of yours. And if you want to pretend our mother didn't run off and leave us and our daddy behind then you can. But I cannot.

"People ought to think more about the consequences of their actions," I said. "They ought to pay attention to how what they're doing hurts others."

"Oh, stop being so dramatic," Darlene said, getting this dreamy look in her eyes then her voice got all soft, which I dreaded because I knew what was coming, "Did I tell you," she asked, "that I saw Jesus in the door of my refrigerator last night? He was on the cross of Calvary. I believe it's a sign."

"A sign of what?" I asked, but she ignored my question as I knew she would. She does when she gets like this. "I had this dream too," she said, "it was your wedding day. You were all in white. I never could bring in the groom. But you, now you were wearing, are you ready for this, you were wearing our mama's wedding dress. You had on her pillbox hat too. And your hair was out to here. God, you looked awesome."

Darlene is off and running. I tune her out and let my own thoughts turn back to Morgan, the meaning of his passing, and the people up in Redjacket.

Vinnie

If I lived in the house without Vinnie this is what I'd do: (1) Burn lights in every room. He wouldn't be here to complain the light bill is too high. (2) Eat Chips Ahoy in bed watching the Tonight Show. Vinnie abhors the Tonight Show. It's really class Vinnie can't stand. It's apparent when you're around Vinnie more than two-seconds. Also, he cannot stomach food being eaten anywhere except in the kitchen. Once, he caught me sitting in the middle of my crushed velvet bed-spread eating a bologna sandwich stacked high with tomato and lettuce, mayonnaise dripping, and he threw up in the toilet. (3) Throw open the windows and let in some air. Vinnie painted the windows shut before Big Daddy died. He won't let me hire someone to unstick them. He fears being robbed in his sleep. I tell him he's safe. You have to have something of value to be robbed and he does not.

But I don't live in the house without Vinnie. So I make do.

I have to make do with other things in my life as well. Like, I have to make do with Jay Leno. Now that Johnny Carson is gone. Johnny was my idol. Sometimes when Jay is on, I push the mute button. Without his voice, Jay is not completely there. I can live with his face. And with the remote in my hand, I can retain some semblance of control.

Then, there is Melinda. Making do with Melinda is hard. Today she and Vinnie are cooking out on the fancy wooden deck Big Daddy had built and enclosed with wooden lattice work. It's only May and already the red roses are in full bloom and creeping up the trellis toward the roof. Big Daddy's hibachi is filled with smoking beef patties.

"Hold the pickles, hold the lettuce, special orders don't upset us," Vinnie sings out into the open air of our yard, his Big Daddy's Chili chef's hat blowing in the wind. Melinda sits in a lawn chair spreading tanning cream on her long lean legs. She wears white shorts and a white tank top from someone else's closet. Someone much smaller, it seems to me.

"Vol-ump-tious," Vinnie says, drawing out the words. He bends to nibble Melinda's ear as though it were the cherry on a sundae.

The sun is beating down on the patio. It is perfect tanning weather. I stretch out on the redwood picnic table in the yard.

"Too bad," I say to Melinda, "Vinnie's bed isn't a *tanning* bed. Hey, Vinnie," I say, laughing to myself at the marvelous line I've just thought up, "get it. A *tanning* bed."

Vinnie gives me a dirty look and turns back to the grill. Melinda tosses the tube of tanning cream on the table and scoots off the recliner to flounce into the kitchen. She returns quickly, not wanting to miss the impending fireworks, with a Bartles and Jaymes, tropical flavor. Her lower lip forms a pout as she sips the cooler through a red and white striped straw.

"You going to look for work?" Vinnie shoots the question in my direction. He hands me a burger on an onion bun and I start slathering it with catsup.

"You ruin everything with catsup," he says, in his whiney ten-year-old voice, "you always did do that. You probably always will."

"Vinnie," I say, "you are a pain in my butt." I eat around the edges of my burger. "I might go to work at the greenhouse on Bixby Road. Working with soil cleanses the soul. Or so I read somewhere."

"That's a career goal?" He moves a chair next to Melinda's. "Drug Mart is hiring."

When I don't answer because my mouth is full of tomato slices, he says, "Drug Mart is hiring." Vinnie is organizing his plate so that nothing touches, a childish hang-up of his. "You know," he says, "someone to stock. So is Sibley's Machine Shop. Inventory. Counting parts."

"Jeez, Vinnie, cut me a break. How many machine parts have you counted in your lifetime? Especially at Sibley's. It's a dump."

"How long do you expect Big Daddy's money to last?"

"Hey, let me worry about that. Counting machine parts! No way, Vinnie!"

Our daddy made it to the big time with his Big Daddy Chili in a can. I'm in charge of his estate. We're all he had left. Me and Vinnie.

Fever rides his motorcycle around the side of the house and before he's completely stopped spinning in the grass, his big black bike vibrating and giving off heat and fumes, I have jumped on behind and am hugging him tight. My haltered breasts crushing into his back. He wears only shorts and tennis shoes.

He laughs and we are gone, flying in the wind, away from Vinnie and Melinda, the house on Berg Avenue with its stuck tight windows, and away from worry about how long Big Daddy's money will last.

"Like Big Daddy," I tell Fever in the softness of his neck, "it will last 'til it's gone."

Macon for Georgia

Larue says I am caught up in clothes which I am not. I cannot say I do not like clothes. I do. They are predictable. Unlike Larue. A red dress is always a red dress.

Now Larue, he can be red-mean one day and blue-moody the next. Or yellow-rotten one day, and green-slimy the day after. Those primary colors are only examples of Larue and how he can be.

Larue has never commented on my shoes and I have nineteen pairs in all. He told me he could remember having only one pair of shoes the whole time he was growing up which when you are doing it seems to go on forever. It could be why Larue never mentions my shoes. He has some endearing ways.

I cannot bear to part with a pair of shoes once they are in my possession. Even if they have outlived their usefulness. Even if they have gone out of style, and the color is all wrong. Oh no! I hang on. That is a major flaw in me. I have never been able to un-root why that is though I have been to see countless therapists and have studied psychology and human behavior. It's a disturbing, annoying trait. A real flaw in me which I will address someday. That is only one of many things I will have to address one day.

I behave the same way in a relationship. A relationship can be over. Dead. Zip. Zero. But I hang on. Even if it becomes stifling, stands still, even peddles backward, I hang on. Even if it becomes terrifying. Well, terrifying is a strong word. I will say disturbing.

Now, Larue is not terrifying. Though I can say there's been times I was scared of him. But not terrified though. Never terrified.

I met Larue at a party. I don't usually go to parties. Not the kind where people get drunk and throw up on expensive furniture that has been especially designed for the house.

This was supposed to be a birthday party for Stevie Burkey who works with me at Drug Mart. Stevie was a person easy to be with. He said he was having his party at a friend's house out in Carrolton's Woods. A place I would never get to see in a million years if I didn't take Stevie up on his invitation. So I did and the rest is history. And I would have been better off not seeing that big beautiful house. I should have left it out in Carrolton Woods or on the pages of Beautiful Homes Magazine. I would have been better off not seeing that house in a million years. Now it is permanently in my mind. Things will never be the same. I know that now.

I parked along the lane leading up to the two-story tudor-style house. It was a good thing. Cars jammed the circular driveway and were parking on the lawn up next to the fountain by the time I left. By then I was a different person than the girl that went through those big double doors a few hours earlier carrying a present for Stevie wrapped in paper that said, "Happy Birthday!" in big red and yellow balloons all over it.

Nobody else brought a present but a few people gathered around Stevie, holding their drinks and making little toasts, while he opened mine.

"I love it, Macon," Stevie said, in a slurred voice, and I could tell he meant it. He held up the label maker which drew laughs from the few people who were paying any attention at all. I knew the label maker was something he wanted. He'd said so when we put it on the shelf at Drug Mart. But he never bought it. He takes home every penny. His mother has cancer. I thought, "Let them laugh. I don't care. Stevie likes it." He was the only person who knew I was named Macon for Georgia and didn't laugh. It's where my mother was from and always wanted to go back to but she died before she had the chance. That was before she ended up in Putnam County, West Virginia, with a husband who wasn't my father. She had gone there looking for my real father but never found him and ended up with a husband she detested. But they are all dead now and it's my policy not to talk about dead people. So I won't. I am here to discuss the living.

I wandered through the house in Carrolton's Woods examining all the fine furniture, some was Ethan Allan which I am up on because I get their catalog, and looking out the dozens of windows. None of them were curtained. The well-lit grounds outside resembled Central Park which I've seen in pictures, with its flowering bushes and little paths going this way and that. I kept running into people everywhere I went in the big house. I got the feeling people were laughing at me and making fun of the label maker. That could have been my paranoia kicking in. When all else fails, I can depend on it to ruin my perception of things.

I was on the second floor sitting in a navy winged-back chair looking at an art book I'd picked up from a glass-topped coffee table.

"Well, lookit what I found!" a tall muscular guy with longish dark hair stood in the doorway. He took a drink from the can of beer in his hand.

Ordinarily I would not talk to a stranger but I said, "Hi." I was feeling out of place there in that big house. Really, I was feeling like the biggest fool in the world for bringing a gift when none was expected. Most people would know that. But no, not me. Not Macon named for Georgia, who will go one step beyond any other living person. Or a million steps if she has to. To make someone like her. To make her like herself.

I had managed in the short span of this party to transfer the feeling I was having to my entire life. I could see only unacceptance and failure both behind and before me when this handsome in a rough-sort-of-way guy, who turned out to be Larue Johnson, grinned at me from the doorway and said, "Ain't you a pretty little thing now." And I guess I was, in my new black sheath dress and my new black pumps. My blond hair was pulled back in a pony tail and tied with a black velvet bow.

Well, I started bawling. I put my head down in my hands and cried off every drop of Magic Mist mascara. I cried like I've never cried before. Larue brought a fluffy sunshine yellow bath towel from the bathroom across the hall which was decorated in these big sunflowers and he dabbed at my eyes. Then he went down to the kitchen and brought back a Pepsi for me and more beer for himself.

We sat and looked at the art book together which was a mistake because it was filled with pictures of nude men and women. I blame everything that happened on that art book.

Larue Johnson caressed me gently at first and then he got somewhat rougher and that's where my memory gets hazy. I believe the Pepsi had something in it. We ended up on the four poster bed across the room which was dressed up in Gloria Vanderbilt sheets and a puffy comforter. The bed was by the French doors looking out on the fountain. It was all lit up. I could hear the water cascading down.

That was the start of our relationship. Which was hot and burning up one minute. And cold as ice the next.

Stevie Burkey brought his label maker to work and we had fun with it. Writing out quotes such as, "It's hard to soar like an eagle when you're working with a bunch of turkeys," and sticking them on work stations.

At home Larue would throw things against the wall, even me when I was handier than a glass or ashtray, and acted out in ways unbecoming a man who had served his country and received a monthly income for injuries sustained doing so.

One day Stevie spelled out the words, "I love you Macon will you marry me?"

I went on stocking shelves. I pretended not to see the label he had stuck across his chest. By then Stevie knew all about Larue.

I ignored Stevie every day for a month while he added new labels to his shirt until his chest was covered with pledges of undying love for me. The messages reminded me of candy hearts. "I'm yours. Be mine."

Then one day Stevie put away the label maker and said seriously, "I love you, Macon, will you marry me?"

I could feel myself breaking up into small pieces. One piece, the piece Stevie held, was a lifeline. I knew it and my heart filled with love for him.

"I have a lot of problems," I said, starting to cry.

"I know," he said in this wise-sounding voice, as he extended his arms to me, "but we have our whole lifetime to work on them."

All I heard was the part where Stevie said, "we." I moved into his gentle embrace.

It was only one step. But it was a beginning.

Ezra

Every day at least once Ezra says, "If I die today, I'm ready." He has said this with conviction for the past six months.

I tell him that he likes his daily cone of Baskin Robbins ice cream too much to die. I also tell him I'm not sure it's the ice cream he likes so much as holding my hand as we walk one block to the ice cream store.

Ezra simply smiles and goes about running the weed eater or whatever tool he happens to be puttering with at the time of our conversation. Besides the weed eater, he's bought from the Kmart on the corner, a red lawn mower, an electric screw driver, a drill, and a number of saws. There are tools in the metal building out back that I don't know the names of.

Ezra sleeps beside me now, his trim body tucked neatly under the smooth lavender sheet. "If you stay in one spot all night," he has confided, "the bed is easier to make."

"Go on and move around," I tell him, "I make the bed now." But, old habits are hard to break. Ezra still sleeps beside me in one spot.

"Maggie," Ezra said, the day of our wedding, "you remind me of a spring flower." I was in my lavender suit. Now Ezra wants everything in our trailer-home lavender, even the padded toilet seat he found at Kmart and installed himself.

"I can kill two birds with one stone," he joked at our wedding, which was on my 60th birthday, a milestone Ezra had already passed. "You know," he grinned, "buy one gift instead of two." We were gathered in Tutti's living room in Columbus.

Tutti, who is Ezra's daughter, was elated we were moving to Florida. "Look at the states I'll drive through coming down," she said. "I can add on to my collection." Tutti has a fetish for plastic water-filled snow scenes. She has one hundred and fifty of these lining her bookshelves.

After our honeymoon, we moved to Trailer Haven outside Orlando. Our place is bordered by palm trees and flowers. I have always wanted to come to Florida. Now my dream has come true. I am living in Paradise.

Ezra says he can live anywhere. That he reckons this place is as good as any. But I see the look in his eye when he is out cutting grass and hears there is a big snow on the ground back in Ohio.

Beside me, Ezra sighs, makes a half turn, then settles on his back, and is quiet.

I swear I see a smile play at his lips. It wouldn't surprise me. A smile is as much a part of Ezra as the OSU ball cap he wears. I am suddenly struck with a sense of urgency to be up and about.

I slip from bed, and pad down the hall to the bathroom. I splash cold water on my face and study my reflection in the mirror.

It was six months ago, on our first date, that I fell in love with Ezra. It's an all-consuming love that makes my heart race, my palms sweaty, and makes me want to be near him. To sleep with him. It was sheer joy to find he felt the same way.

We lived all our lives in Ohio, not thirty miles apart. When I ask Ezra what he did all those years, he swears he was frozen in time waiting for me. He says those things and I tell him he's foolish. But he has changed my life.

"I can whip the world," I tell him as I climb behind the wheel of the pickup.

"You and who else?" He asks, swinging in beside me. But I see admiration in those clear blue eyes.

In the kitchen, I wipe a fleck of dust from the glass-topped table, and pick a single crumb from the seat of one of the beige velour swivel chairs. It is the finest kitchen set I've ever owned.

I measure coffee and water into the coffee machine and sit on one of the beige velour chairs while it drips. I squirt coconut lotion into the palm of my hand from the bottle on the counter. The scent of coconut lotion takes me back to our honeymoon in Hawaii. We went with a tour group.

"Not cheap," Ezra tells people, "but worth every penny."

On the plane, we were served fancy shrimp dinners and Mai Tais by beautiful girls in flowered muu muus. Hawaiian music played in the background. We could have gone home right then and been content.

By the time we got to the Hyatt hotel with gardenia lei's and a 5x7 picture someone took of us, Ezra smiling and holding my hand, I was delirious with happiness. From the window of our room we could see palm trees swaying in the warm breeze, a group of children laughing by the pool, and in the distance, the vast blue ocean.

"If I die tomorrow, I'll die happy," Ezra sighed. We were just back from sightseeing. He had kicked off his shoes, unbuttoned his silk shirt, and was stretched out on the bed.

That was when he started this I'm-ready-to-die stuff.

"This is all a bonus, you know," he waved his arm around the luxurious hotel room. I was curling my hair on pink rollers.

"You literally saved me from dying," he said. "I was dying, you know. My heart is wore out. So if this is the grand finale, it's okay by me."

I went on twisting gray hair around a pink roller. I refused to think of Ezra dying. We had to much to do to die. We were planning the big move to Florida.

I got Ezra out of his mood by slicing a pineapple. Sitting at the table with me, eating the juicy spears, he forgot everything but that we were on our honeymoon. Later, we went out for Baskin Robbins ice cream.

I rub more lotion on my hands and work it around the cuticles. That was all we brought back from the island. The coconut lotion, our memories, and Tutti's souvenirs. Two water-filled snow scenes. A hula girl and a palm tree. And a boy on a surf board.

The laughter of a child interrupts my thoughts. Through the window I see a small pony-tailed girl chasing a red ball across our lawn.

The ball bounces against the life-size deer Ezra brought with him from Ohio. Pony-tail flying, the little girl scoops up her ball and is gone.

"People down here will love this thing," Ezra said as we unloaded the deer from his pickup. I was trying to hold most of the deer's weight because of his heart.

I never let on about his heart. The only time I did, we were carrying in the glass-topped table. We bought it at an estate sale down the coast.

With the table in his hand, Ezra had to stop and lean against the doorway. He was having trouble breathing. I pulled up a chair for him. That was when he protested.

"Forget my heart, you hear, Maggie! Just forget my heart!"

And, for the most part, I have tried to forget. To forget that the doctor warned another attack is imminent. Sometimes I can go a full day without it entering my mind. Then, there it is, black as night, and I have to creep to the bathroom to splash cold water on my face.

I glance out the window again and my eyes light on the deer standing there in the midst of Ezra's flower garden. He was right. Everyone in the trailer park has stopped by at one time or another to comment on that deer.

The smell of coffee has filled the kitchen. I get out two mugs and add coffee, cream, and sugar. I place two lavender napkins on the new bed tray from Kmart.

I take extra time arranging the tray. I start down the hall and turn back. I add a lavender flower from the arrangement on the TV. I am careful not to stumble on the wrinkle in the hall carpet.

"You fall and break your leg," Ezra has joked, "and I'll be up a creek, woman." He tells everyone how I wait on him. But, really, it's the other way around.

The mugs start to slide and the coffee nearly spills. I steady the tray. "More than anything," I confided to my friend, Isabel, one morning in the pickup, "Ezra loves his morning coffee."

"Not as much as I love you, Maggie," he blurted out, right in front of Isabel. He jammed his OSU ball cap down on his head and pulled out into the stream of traffic on the corner of our street.

Isabel sometimes joins us on our trips down the coast. She brings a container of piping hot coffee and a bag of powdered-sugar donuts. We leave when it's daylight and stop for breakfast along the way. That was a special day, the day we found the glass-topped table and swivel chairs.

"Oh, go on," I said to Ezra, who winked at me as Isabel poured coffee into a white foam cup. I felt my face go red and my heart start beating faster. While Isabel sipped coffee and stared out the window at an orange grove, I edged closer to him and rubbed his arm with my finger until I saw goose bumps appear. He was grinning from ear to ear.

In our bedroom, I set the tray on the dresser and cross the room to open the curtains. I see a light rain falling. It splashes off the building where Ezra stores his tools. The faintest rainbow appears in the sky.

"Sleepy head," I say softly, turning toward the bed. "It's time to get up."

I note the corners of Ezra's lips are still turned up in a slight smile. But, he doesn't move. Somehow I knew he wouldn't.

the end

Vada Faith

Chapter One

"I'm going to be a surrogate mother," I said, positioning the pink salon chair so my twin sister, Joy Ruth, could see her hair in the mirror. I made the announcement calmly, as if my knees were not shaking. I held on to the back of the chair for support.

My sister's eyes popped open, wider than I'd ever seen them, and she froze for a few seconds.

I held my breath. The air between us was as charged as a new battery. The secret that I'd kept inside me for too long was now out.

"A surrogate mother!" She squealed as if I'd squirted her with bug spray instead of the expensive hair spray I held in my hand.

"Yes," I said, letting the air out of my lungs slowly. "A surrogate mother."

I gave her hair another good misting.

"A surrogate mother?" She repeated, her eyes still frozen in place.

"Yes, I'm thinking about having a baby for a couple who can't have a child of their own."

I gave her hair another generous misting of hair spray, hoping she hadn't noticed my shaking hands.

"Stop!" Joy Ruth waved at the gathering mist. "Your tubes are tied." She blinked several times, her eyes finally working. She shook her head in puzzlement. "Your tubes have been tied since the twins were born." She turned to face me. "You said you'd never give birth again in this life." She grasped the arms of the chair as if she were experiencing air turbulence on a plane instead of sitting right there in a chair in our beauty salon. "You're teasing. Right? Vada Faith?"

I ignored her and grabbed the blow dryer, aiming it at a clump of her blonde hair on the pink counter.

"Are you trying to make medical history?" She fanned herself with her hand, and sighed. "I can see the headlines now. Woman with tied tubes gives birth to ten pound baby girl." She turned back to her reflection in the mirror and stared into my eyes. "Oh, my God! You mean it, don't you, Vada Faith?" A stricken look came across her face. She whipped around to stare at me. "You mean you'd have a baby and give it away? Have you lost your mind?"

I went to the closet and grabbed the pink broom she had found at the Dollar Store and started sweeping her blonde hair into a pile. I had enough on my mind without her throwing a hissy fit.

Thankfully, her eyes wandered back to her own reflection but this was news she couldn't ignore. She turned back to me and shook her head in total disbelief. "Have a baby and give it away?"

"Go on," I said, busying myself by straightening the counter in front of me, "make this difficult for me. I knew you would."

I put the hair dryer back in the rack and brought out a stack of new magazines and placed them on the counter. It was getting so we had to cater to our customers.

"Don't you have Country Stars Mag?" Midgy Brown had asked only yesterday.

I wanted to say, "Like we need to know what country singers are doing every two seconds." Instead I rushed across the street to Phillips Drug Store and bought the latest issue until we could get a subscription ordered.

"Did I say I am a surrogate mother today, Joy Ruth?" I fanned the new magazines out so our customers could see the selection. "No! I did not. I said I am thinking about it. In the future, Joy Ruth. In the future. There's a big difference here. Besides, I've decided to have that tube surgery reversed."

"Why would you go and do a thing like that? You said you didn't want more kids." She fluffed her bangs and ran her fingers back through her long blonde hair.

I'd been trying to persuade her to let me give her a stylish short cut ever since we graduated from beauty school. An inch was the most she'd let me cut. She still wore her hair the way she had in high school.

"I don't want any more kids." I ran my fingers through my own short blonde hair. This was worse than explaining something to my two little girls. "I would be having a baby for the Kilgores."

"The who?" Her eyebrows shot up into two dark arches over her blue eyes.

I'd never noticed before how dark her eyebrows were. Mine were much lighter. Another difference between us.

"The Kilgores." I picked up a comb and ran it through my bangs, which were wispy and totally unlike Joy Ruth's. I kept my hair short and simple. The way I tried to keep my life.

Lately, though, it didn't seem to be working.

I sighed. I was tired of repeating everything to her. It seemed that was my role in life. "They built that big house out on the mountain. It's where the old Sherman place used to be."

Telling my sister about wanting to be a surrogate mother was harder than I'd thought it would be. Almost as hard as trying to make the decision itself. I had hoped for her support. Who was I kidding. I knew deep down, I'd never win her over on this one.

"Good Lord!" She squealed. "Why would you have a baby for them? Isn't he the guy with the tan? The one I see in the mall in those skimpy nylon running shorts? His wife's always tagging along behind. The Barbie doll look alike."

"They're good people," I said, taking the scissors and snipping a flyaway hair from her head. I tried not to think of Roy Kilgore in his tiny running shorts or of Dottie Kilgore who really did look like she belonged in a cardboard package with a cellophane front. I was already too far into this thing to have any negative thoughts. Any thoughts at all that kept me from looking anywhere but straight ahead. Yep. It was too late. I was already into this thing knee-deep. I had given my word to the Kilgores.

"Will you put those scissors down," she snapped, reaching up and taking them from me. "Look here." She placed the scissors on the counter.

I could feel the storm clouds gathering as I faced her.

"I know some good people," she said, in her prissy voice, "but you don't see me having babies for them. Are you crazy?" Her face bunched up into a frown and her eyes narrowed. "Is there something I don't know? Are you having an affair with Roy Kilgore? Is that what this is about?" She stared down at her denim capris.

"No!" I fell into a chair beside her. "I can't believe you said that." I looked down at my own denim capris. Our pants matched perfectly. How could we dress alike without ever discussing it? Twin syndrome. It drove me nuts.

"Well, then, are your hormones out of whack? Are you going through the change? What's going on?"

"I have not cracked up." I could see my pale face in the mirror. "I am not going through the change. Thank you." It was like her to blame it on menopause, the big topic among the women in our salon.

I had decided to tell her about the surrogacy today because it was Monday and the shop was closed. We usually spent the day bringing the books up to date, doing our hair and nails, and catching up with the details of our personal lives.

I studied my tanned arms where I'd smoothed on some Estee Lauder tanning cream earlier. "Maybe a change," I finally answered her question, "but not the one you're referring to. I want to do something significant with my life. I want to do something for someone else. Besides, I have to think about the future. The Kilgores will pay fifty-thousand dollars to whoever carries their baby, plus expenses, and anything else the surrogate might need or want." I reached over to the pump on the counter and squirted some coconut hand cream into my hands.

"It's not just about money, though," I said, "I've thought it all through and I really want to do this for them. Besides," I sighed, "where else could I get that kind of money? The way things are now I'm never going to get that new house I want. By the time I save a down payment, the beautiful house I want in Crystal Springs will be gone. I don't happen to have a stock portfolio like you."

As the words left my mouth I knew I'd stepped over the line.

My sister gave me a dirty look. She hated it when I referred to the money she received from a car accident in high school. Thankfully, she wasn't hurt and she'd invested some of the settlement in the shop. She even put my name up out front so that I'd know we truly were partners. I was grateful to her for that.

However, she was judgmental with a capital J. I expected to see Judge Joy Ruth have her own TV show any day.

"Can I help it if some old man rear ended the car I was riding in?" She dipped a cotton ball into polish remover and with great swipes started cleaning off her red nail polish. "Can I help it that the guy was a bank president and he gave me a big settlement just for being there in the back seat of Jo Dee Rendell's car? So, I doubled it in investments. Are you doing this to get even?"

"No way," I said. "I have to help myself. I'm the unlucky one."

"Unlucky!" She raised her eyebrows in shock. "You're the luckiest person I know. You've got John Wasper's old family home place. So it's not new. Big deal."

That was my sister's line. Big deal.

"I'd love to have that old Victorian place," she rambled on rubbing the cotton ball furiously over her nails. "Look at its history. How many houses in this town can claim Eleanor Roosevelt had tea on the front porch? I'd take it off your hands in a minute." She sighed deeply. "You have a husband who dotes on you, two beautiful little girls. Unlucky? Lord, girl, grow up." She got this disgusted look on her face which meant she was thinking up more mean things to say as she finished cleaning off her nail polish.

All through school, I had drifted along on dreams of being rescued by a handsome prince. That he galloped into my life as my playmate John Wasper Waddell, carrying a football and wearing a cougar uniform, was all the more wonderful. I was swept away on the wild horse of his undying affection and for years we had lived in wedded bliss.

Somewhere over the years my life had seemed to stop. It had bogged down in a rut of ordinariness.

I studied my profile in the mirror. I leaned close and examined my teeth to see if the new whitening toothpaste was working. I decided my sister could think whatever she wanted. I ran my tongue over my white teeth. I wasn't feeling lucky today. It was true. She was always in the right place at the right time. Oh, I was considered the prettier twin - though the mirror told me we looked alike. I might be a little more stylish. My sister didn't care much about fashion or style. I'd learned a long time ago looks were not everything.

It was my sister who had dated John Wasper first but it was he and I who were true soul mates. One Saturday afternoon he was late coming over to go with Joy Ruth to the library and she left without him. He never did make it. Instead he sat down beside me on the back porch steps and before either of us knew it the fireflies were out and we were holding hands. After that, it was as if the two of them had never dated. There was no keeping us apart. I was paper and he was the flame.

My sister never let on that she cared. I knew she did. She hung around us with this moonstruck look on her face whenever he'd come to see me.

After we married and had the girls her infatuation seemed to fade. I couldn't help but wonder if deep down she still cared for him and if that wasn't why she'd never married. She'd had some serious relationships over the years but had broken them all off.

In school she'd hung out with the brainy crowd and I'd hung out with the popular group. Girls the boys gave their hearts to. I was home-coming queen and voted the prettiest girl in our senior class. Joy Ruth had been voted the most likely to succeed.

Most of the school papers posted on our avocado green refrigerator had belonged to my sister, my straight A sister. Daddy had put them right next to a West Virginia University banner. She ignored his hint and joined me at the beauty school in Charleston.

Now, it was time for me to make a change. I stood up and started putting supplies away.

I was about to do something so monumental I almost exploded with the enormity of it, being a surrogate mother for someone. This was beyond anything I'd ever imagined doing and it sent an excitement cursing through my veins unlike anything I'd ever felt and, although I wanted that new house in Crystal Springs in a big way, I wanted to be a surrogate more. Having a new house paled in comparison to helping two people realize their dream of becoming parents.

Carrying a baby for this couple had appealed to me from the start and the more I thought about it the more I wanted to do it. My life was already taking on new meaning and it surpassed anything I'd experienced. I was ready to move forward. Fast.

The shop was quiet now except for the drip of the faucet in the back bathroom. Even the radio was silent. Without Carrie Underwood singing, "Jesus take the Wheel," or Vince Gill crooning one of his sweet melodies, it was like a tomb. I had hoped our conversation about surrogacy would be easier than it was turning out to be, but that was me. Always thinking everything was going to be easier than it really was. I wished it was Tuesday and Vada Faith's Beauty Bar was full of customers. I was beginning to hate Mondays and my time alone with my sister.

I went into the reception area and retrieved the caramel truffle coffee I'd brought in earlier. Back at my station, I drank it slowly and tossed the cup into the waste can.

"You don't know these people, honey," Joy Ruth said, examining her nails. She turned back to the mirror and smoothed on some lip gloss. "Who are they anyway? Where'd you find them? I mean, they show up here from only the Lord knows where. They buy some land," she ran her tongue across her teeth, a reflex from the lip gloss, "build a new house and now, wham-o, you're going to have a baby for them. A baby, Vada Faith. A real live little baby. Like one of your precious twins. A little human being."

"I've thought it all through. You don't seem to understand that a surrogacy baby would never be mine. It would belong to Roy and Dottie Kilgore. Right from its conception." I came to stand behind her, staring into the same mirror with her. "Didn't the Virgin Mary give her son, Jesus, to the world? Well, that is exactly what I would be doing. It's something I want to do more than anything else. Can't you try to understand, for me?"

When she frowned, I picked up my tote bag and started loading it with supplies to take home.

"This is not about the Virgin Mary," she snapped. "Have you forgotten about your husband. What about John Wasper? What does he say about all this?"

"I have not forgotten him. I'll tell him when the time comes." I closed my tote bag and went over to the Coke machine. I put in some coins and punched a button. The Coke fell with a bang.

"When the time comes?" She stood up and folded her arms in front of her. "You mean you haven't even told your husband what you want to do? Well, the time has come, girl. You're nuts. You said being pregnant was no picnic. You liked giving birth even less. Now help me figure this out."

"No matter what I do, you're against me." I opened the Coke and took a long drink. Like some of her words, it burned going down. "It makes no difference what I do, even if I think of changing my eye shadow you say it's a mistake."

"This is not eye shadow we're talking about here, little sister."

"Don't call me little sister. I am your age. Exactly." I was so mad I could spit nails. I wasn't stupid. I knew it was time to discuss it with my husband. I just hadn't figured out how.

"You," she said, pointing her finger at me, "were born one minute after me, therefore, you are my little sister."

"So for that I have to pay for the rest of my life. You are not my boss. I hate you sometimes, Joy Ruth. Lately I hate you a lot."

"The feeling is mutual."

I grabbed my "Shop 'til I Drop" tote bag and slammed out of the shop. Miss High and Mighty could finish the inventory and close up by herself. I was mad as a hornet. She was being a pain in the butt. I was mad at myself too. For letting her get to me. For knowing she was right about talking it over with John Wasper sooner. Just when I'd thought things in my life were about to get better.

I set off down the street, furious at the world for not being perfect.

I didn't look back as I hurried away. I knew Joy Ruth was standing in the doorway watching me. It was out of character for me to leave upset. I always wanted to work things out, especially with her. Well, she could just get used to things being different between us.

It was time to cut the cord which had thickened between us when mama walked off and left us. Sure, she left us with our daddy. However, two little girls needed a mama more than they needed anything else.

I headed down Main Street at a fast clip, the tote bag slapping at my legs. The sun beat down on the top of my head. I could feel a trickle of perspiration beginning at my hairline. I wished now I'd driven to work. I wasn't in any mood to amble through City Park the way I usually did, enjoying the flowers and listening to the birds.

Thoughts of mama leaving us in that run-down trailer with daddy ran through my mind like a bad movie.

"Yoo hoo, Vada Faith!" I turned at the familiar voice.

I shaded my eyes and looked across the street. Midgy Brown stood on the corner pushing her frizzy red hair out of her eyes.

"Hey," I said. While she was a good friend and steady customer I wasn't in the mood to talk to her about her latest country heartthrob or about her latest cause. She was always heading up some committee to save something.

Nope, today, I had my own problems to think about and nobody was going to help me. Nobody but me, myself, and I.

Chapter Two

My very first lesson in small town dynamics came the summer I met John Wasper Waddell.

It was hot that afternoon, the day he and his big brother Bruiser, and his younger brother Bobby Joe, rode up in front of our trailer on brand new bikes. Bruiser put down his shiny kick stand and yelled from the middle of the yard, "Hey, you twins. You wanna build a fort?"

John Wasper and Bobby Joe had hopped off their bikes and stood beside him staring across the yard at us.

It was almost too good to be true. There were no kids on our road and most days Joy Ruth and I were left to amuse ourselves.

"Yes," Joy Ruth and I screamed in unison, "we wanna build a fort."

We jumped from the front porch steps where we'd been fighting over the comics and raced to meet them, tripping over our flip flops as we went. We showed the boys the creek that ran along the back of the property. They promptly jumped in and splashed us until our shorts and shirts clung to our skinny bodies like Saran Wrap and our blond hair hung in strings. We didn't care.

When their backs were turned we pushed them into the creek and fell in behind them, laughing and splashing.

That was the beginning of our friendship. The boys came nearly every day after that and we spent hours hammering tree houses and forts and building dams in the creek to keep the turtles and frogs from escaping.

If only we'd kept to that simple routine.

However, we got bored and started making the long trek into town to the A & P for a candy bar. I was the only one who bought a different kind of candy bar each time.

The day I bought my first Baby Ruth was when it happened.

I had the candy bar in my hand and was pulling change from the pocket of my red seersucker shorts, anticipating the taste of chocolate and peanuts on my tongue. I got into the check-out line, leaving Joy Ruth and the boys to make their decisions. I was eager to peel off the red and white wrapper and take my first bite of the fat chocolate bar.

"I might just start calling Joy Ruth Baby Ruth," I thought as I waited. I looked back at her, acting cool, flipping her hair in John Wasper's cute boy face. She would hate being called baby anything. She thought being born one minute before me made her the oldest sister. The more superior.

Daddy said it didn't. He said I might have been born first except Joy Ruth was wrapped so tightly around me she caused me to be blue and they had to pull her out first. He said she squealed for an hour after they untangled us. Then when they put us together in the same crib he said we snuggled up like two peas in a pod.

"Hello, Vada Faith," Miss Wright had said that summer day at the A & P, looking down at me as she rang up my candy bar. I learned from her name badge that her whole name was Miss Emily Wright. I only knew her as Miss Wright. She taught Bible school every summer at the Tabernacle Holiness Church on Park Street which wasn't close enough for us to walk to but we did anyway.

"Hello, Miss Wright," I said. She peered down at me with her big milky eyes, magnified by thick glasses framed in tortoise shell.

She turned to Miss Dunkel who ran the register beside her and jerked her permed head toward me. "Bea," she said, nodding, "this is Vada Faith. One of the Dunn twins."

I knew Miss Bea Dunkel too. She served cupcakes at Bible school from the kitchen in the church basement and she got mad if you got crumbs on the floor.

"I know Vada Faith," Miss Dunkel said to Miss Wright, her eyes never leaving her register. She stared over half glasses that hung by a rhinestone chain around her skinny neck.

When Miss Wright held out my change, I could have been a mechanical doll wrapping my fingers around the cold coins for all the heed she paid me. I turned to go.

"Helena and Delbert's girl," Miss Wright said, snapping her words off like breaking crackers. "Hel-e-na Car-ter." She started talking loudly as if Miss Dunkel had ear wax build up.

"Oh, Helena, yes," Miss Dunkel said. She sounded as if she and my mother were best friends and that she had the inside scoop. Well, my mama was a mystery. Even I knew that.

"Helena always fancied herself higher up the totem pole than us." Miss Dunkel's voice sounded again. "Then doesn't she marry that handsome Delbert Dunn. He didn't have the best reputation. Just the best body."

"You mean Doolittle Dunn?" Miss Wright's fingers hit the register keys with a clang as she checked items for the man who'd stood behind me. She had put special emphasis on Daddy's nickname. Doo-little.

"Well, Helena ran off and left them," Bea's voice rose to a high pitch. "So poor Delbert can't hold a regular job raising those wild girls. I feel so sorry for him."

I was nearing the door, fighting back tears. The Wheaties I'd had earlier that morning were threatening to slide back up my throat. How could they say such awful things?

My enthusiasm for the candy bar was gone.

"It's a cryin' shame," Miss Wright said, "a real cryin' shame."

I made it outside before the tears came. I swallowed hard and threw the Baby Ruth into the trash barrel on the sidewalk. Through the big plate glass window of the A & P, I could see Miss Wright and Miss Dunkel ringing up other customers.

I ran across the parking lot as fast as I could go, covering my ears to try to stop Miss Wright's voice going around in my head.

I wanted to shut out the truth in her words. Our mama had left us and our daddy didn't have a job. I knew all that.

I refused to let anyone see me cry. Not Joy Ruth who thought our life was fine and certainly not John Wasper whose boy face I had already begun to love.

Behind me, John Wasper started calling out, "Hey, Vada Faith. Wait up, you hear. Wait up. Vada Faith?"

Years later, I would wait many times over for Mr. James John "Wasper" Waddell but not that day. I kept on running, my red canvas tennis shoes hitting the hot pavement, driving the heat right up into my feet and through the rest of my body until it came to rest on the top of my head like hot coals.

I ran as if all the demons in Hell were after me.

I looked over my shoulder only once to see John Wasper and Joy Ruth in earnest conversation, their heads bent together, munching on the candy bars they'd bought. Bruiser and Bobby Joe lagged behind licking chocolate from their fingers.

Even though Joy Ruth and John Wasper stared at the candy bars longer than any of us, the two of them always picked a Hershey with Almonds. They said you always knew what you were getting when you got a Hershey with Almonds.

To this day, those two will not try anything new or different and certainly not anything controversial.

On the other hand, I, Vada Faith, was always up for something new. Back then and now. Something different. Even if I ended up hating it, I was always willing to give it a try.

I slammed into the trailer that summer day, past daddy stretched out on the sofa reading the newspaper, and buried myself in the sweet smell of the patchwork quilt covering the small bed I shared with my sister.

We didn't have much, but daddy kept everything we had clean, especially the bedding. He was home most days and he was always running the old washer out on the built-in porch, hanging clothes on the clothesline strung between two posts out behind the trailer.

I can see him to this day with several clothespins stuck in his mouth hanging a row of our worn pink panties on the line to dry in the sun.

"Hey," Daddy said, coming to stand in the doorway as I lay sobbing on the bed. "You all right, Vada Faith?"

It was his standard question.

"I'm all right," I said, sniffling, giving my standard answer.

"Okay." He stood there a minute more, looking uncomfortable, then he trudged back to his newspaper.

Problem solved.

Well, not entirely.

A seed of longing was forming deep inside me. A longing to be something more than I was. To be someone special. Someone everybody looked up to.

That day I just wiped away my tears and joined the others in the backyard.

At the edge of the woods there was a big competition going on. The prize was the extra Hershey bar John Wasper had bought. The person who could climb to the top of the old Maple tree won the candy bar.

I knew I could win hands down. I was the best climber in the bunch and the most daring.

Besides I was motivated. My Baby Ruth rested at the bottom of the trash can at the A & P. And I was hungry for chocolate.

Summary of Vada Faith

This is a fun new novel set in a beauty shop in the fictional town of Shady Creek, West Virginia. Follow the antics of shop owners Vada Faith Waddell and her feisty twin sister, Joy Ruth. When Vada Faith signs on to be a surrogate mother to earn a downpayment for a big home in the fancy new subdivision of Crystal Springs, she learns too late that the childless couple, Dottie and Roy Kilgore, are small time criminals.

When Vada Faith loses the support of her beloved husband, John Wasper, she realizes that in pursuing her own selfish dreams, she's about to lose everything she's ever held dear. Her two little girls being bullied at school is the last straw. She knows she has to put a stop to the avalanche of hurt she's caused. The question is how? And what does she do about the little baby she carries? This is a serious yet humorous story of complicated relationships and solid family values.

Praise for Vada Faith

"When her impulsive decision to become a surrogate mother turns out to be a terrible mistake, Vada Faith finds herself in the middle of a storm. No matter what she does, someone will be hurt. In her debut novel, Barbara Whittington has created an outspoken, lovable character, filled with dreams, who will make you laugh and cry. If you like books that explore the human heart, you'll love being with Vada Faith as she decides what is important in her life. I know I did."
By: Elizabeth Vollstadt

"It was great to read Vada Faith, a story rife with dangers and potential disaster for all who surround Vada Faith, a small-town wife who has out-of-the-ordinary aspirations. Her choices affect all who are close to her. The book moves with witty and crisp detail and dialogue and has several reenforcing themes about family, relationships, and life.

I love the humor in the book, the personality of Vada Faith and her quips and under-the-breath comments, attention to detail (make up, what people are wearing--hysterical) and the interconnectedness of people no matter who they are. A strong, knock-you-in-the-head theme is how important the unborn life is.

The author's style is crisp, heavy on witty, detailed dialogue and not so much on long narrative. It makes the book move quickly. The short chapters give a feel of a play with scenes. With the dialogue, one could act out the chapters on stage. The author's ability to describe the every-day events and people in a small town is wonderful. I wanted to guess how the book would end, but I did not. What a great read."
By: Thomas A. Donlon, III

"I love this book. I found the characters well-developed, believable -and lovable. I can emphathize with the main character as she finds herself in challenging dilemmas as she searches in all the wrong places for identity and meaning to her life, only to realize she has everything she needs to be happy as well as what is truly important. I keep re-reading it!"
By: Kyleann Williams

Barbara Whittington, an award winning author, native of Putnam County, West Virginia, currently lives with her husband Raymond in a small rural town in Ohio. Ezra and Other Stories is Barbara's second book. Her first novel Vada Faith is available on Amazon in both paperback and Kindle versions. Her work has appeared in The Plain Dealer, Charleston Gazette, and Christian Science Monitor, Women's World, and many others places.

Barbara is available to do book signings, for speaking about her writing, and about her love of books. She will participate in book club discussions of her book via email.
Contact her at barbwhitti@aol.com. Use the title of her book as the subject. Check out her blog at www.barbwhitti.blogspot.com.

A few of her favorite authors are: Maeve Binchy (The Scarlet Feather), Elizabeth Berg (What we Keep), Anne Tyler (Digging to America), Jeanne Ray (Eat Cake), and Southern writer Lee Smith whose entire body of work has been a guiding force for Barbara's own writing. She says her favorite author is usually the one whose book she is reading at the time.

Sweet Baby James

Sequel to Vada Faith

Coming Soon!

www.ingramcontent.com/pod-product-compliance
Lightning Source LLC
Chambersburg PA
CBHW060131260626
47160CB00005B/2071